Art of Vengeance

by Mel J. McNairy

 Filibuster Press, Elkhart, Indiana

Art of Vengeance

by Mel J. McNairy

Published by:
Filibuster Press
55836 Riverdale Drive
Elkhart, Indiana 46514-1112

Library of Congress Catalog Card Number: 97-76807
ISBN: 0-9644007-6-6

0987654321

Cover design by Gregory R. Miller, Indianapolis, Indiana

To my wife Linda who believed in me when it counted most and enhanced my work with her wisdom and skills. I couldn't have done it without you.
And to our dearest friend Bonnie who devoted many hours of her short life to help a cop chase a dream.

ONE

A computer screen inside "A" Building at Stockford Station suddenly beeped to life, causing Sparkey to instinctively roll his chair closer, then adjust his keyboard. Data began flashing across the screen faster than even the lieutenant's practiced eyes could follow. "It lives! It lives!" Sparkey said in his best Dr. Frankenstein voice, while clasping and rubbing his hands together like a mad scientist on the brink of success.

Five feet of chain ran from his wrist to an iron plate on his desk. It allowed some freedom but also guaranteed he would always be in position whenever circumstances dictated. The information he received was never likely to alter the course of world events, but it involved some of the best-kept secrets the military had to offer.

Lieutenant Curtis, or Sparkey as the other six men on his crew called him, punched several keys on the keyboard while quietly whistling the Jetsons' theme song.

Sergeant Kennedy turned from an array of keyboards and lights to look at his lieutenant, whose normally handsome face was now intentionally distorted to fit his mad scientist routine. Kennedy, the oldest of seven men locked inside "A" Building, chuckled, shook his head and turned back to scan the screen in front of him.

"What've we got tonight Sparkey?" he asked without

looking away from the monitors. "Anything?"

"Well, let's take a look," came the reply in Lieutenant Curtis' normal voice. He punched in the electronic combination that unlocked and opened a door on a small safe just to the left of his computer screen.

"All right gentlemen!" Sparkey said, as he finished loading the disk and reviewing their new orders. "We get to talk to the stars tonight."

Day and night, like a giant bionic ear, the large satellite dish at the Stockford Army Station tuned in on conversations far above the earth's atmosphere. Not verbal conversations, but digital messages between satellites and transmitters. Stockford was one of eighteen U.S. monitoring stations around the world responsible for gathering all signals transmitted to or received from any satellite orbiting the planet. These signals were fed through filters to highly advanced computers where the nature of any transmission was identified and recorded. Tonight Sparkey's data apparently indicated that something demanded his crew's attention.

"So we finally get to do some talkin'," drawled a large sergeant with short cropped blond hair. With a good pinch of his favorite chewing tobacco tucked neatly in his jaw, the sergeant finished making a line on a large clear glass board in the middle of the room. There were permanent markings on the board that made up a map of some sort, but unlike any road map or atlas ever seen. Including its heavy wooden base, the glass map stood seven feet tall and was almost thirty feet long. The six-foot ten-inch Texan spit a mouthful of brown juice into an olive-green rations can, being careful to lean forward so as not to soil his crisp clean army fatigues.

"How 'bout it, Lieutenant?" he asked, adjusting his gun belt and .45 automatic. "Anything good?"

"Hang on, Tex." The lieutenant held up his right hand as he continued to read the orders from his screen.

In addition to the lieutenant, Tex and Sergeant Kennedy, there were two communications specialists on duty, Mark and Juan, who could be seen through the glass map, sitting at their posts while wearing their headphones. Each of the men had one side of his headset slightly off the ear so he could pick up on most of the conversations in the room.

Beside the vault-like door into the large control room sat the electronics technician. He was carefully soldering a connection on the back of a circuit board that had been pulled from its place inside one of the control boxes. Just outside the large door was a long hallway. At the end of the hall was a security desk with eight video screens displaying the views of several cameras that covered most of the angles around and in "A" Building. In addition to screening all personnel who attempted to enter the building, the lone M.P. who sat at this station was also responsible for the door alarms and the main control room.

Outside, other heavily armed military police and K-9 patrols completed the formidable Stockford security detail. Except for the large satellite antenna and the roaming guards, Stockford maintained a fairly low profile. Its four simple buildings could almost pass as one of the several Central Indiana farms in the area.

Standing in his darkened bedroom, looking over the grounds, was a nightly ritual for Colonel John Freedman. His assignment as commander of Stockford Station was crucial to national security, but, nonetheless, somewhat mundane.

The experienced fifty-year-old colonel was looking forward to retirement in eight months. He looked down on his nightstand at his digital clock. Eleven thirty-four ... over a half-hour later than his normal bedtime, but tonight he was not even sleepy. The colonel checked to make sure his alarm was set and placed it back between the two phones that shared the top of the nightstand. One phone was black. It was used every night to call his wife in Oklahoma. The other phone, red, had never been used as far as the colonel knew. He lay back in his bed on top of the covers with his arms behind his head. Something was wrong. He just had no idea what it was.

The guard inside "A" Building, down the hall from the control room, held one of several telephones to his head. "Yes sir, we have an all clear on one through eight." He wedged the receiver between his shoulder and ear while using both hands to flip and check a series of switches in a routine that had obviously been performed many times before. "Sir, outside is a check ... Inside checks and infrared is on and quiet. Yes sir. Whiskey, Tango." He snapped his operating initials and returned the receiver to the hook.

"Delta, Charley," Sparkey replied from his chained position in the control room. Of the three phones to the left of his desk, none of them had dials. Sparkey hung up one of two black phones. The third was red and unused. "OK! Here we go!" Sparkey raised his voice so that all could hear. "It looks like our guys have stumbled across a build-up of some hardware in the middle of a desert in Egypt somewhere. We currently don't have anything focused in that area, so we have to talk to one of our stars about takin' a few pictures for us."

Talking to the stars was a Stockford term for transmitting specially coded messages to one of several military satellites in orbit around the earth. These messages could be as simple as the one Lieutenant Curtis' team was about to send or as complex as activating an attack-capable satellite. The men and women at Stockford Security Base knew very well that laser-firing spacecraft not only existed but had been called upon during certain military conflicts.

"Our host for this evening," Sparkey continued, "is Delta, Mike, three, zero, niner, Delta, Charley."

As the identification numbers of the satellite were read off, Sergeant Kennedy's fingers danced across the keyboards on his console. "Stand by." He paused, then began reading from a screen above his head. "OK Tex, two, four, niner at seven, seven, one."

The Texan scanned along the top of the glass map and then made a small mark with his grease pencil. He quickly ran his finger down the middle and marked a second point. "Well, gawd damn," Tex said, as he connected the two points. "They could 'av given us a little bit more time. This thang's damn near outta our range."

"We've gotta give it a shot," Sparkey said. "Where's that ol' team spirit?"

Tex shook his head as he placed a huge protractor on a line that ran the length of the map. "We need a zero four niner at about two seven two."

Sparkey leaned out as far as the chain around his wrist would allow, to look at a small corporal across the room whose uniform looked as if it belonged to a big brother. Corporal Beck, the unit's electronics technician, dialed the proper adjustment with his right hand, while holding an apple in his left. Atop the corporal's head was a set of Mickey Mouse ears.

"Geez! I feel like one of the seven dwarfs in here!" Sparkey smiled as he spoke to Sergeant Kennedy a few feet away.

"Hey, Mickey!" the lieutenant said louder to the tiny soldier across the room. "Are we all set, Mr. Mouse?"

"No problem, Lieutenant," the corporal said over his shoulder while tapping a key on the keyboard beside him.

The whole building shook as powerful motors turned and aimed the giant satellite dish that rumbled to life from its rest over "A" Building. Except for the computers, the building fell silent again. Corporal Beck checked some readings, then gave a thumbs-up sign.

Tex nervously spit another mouthful of tobacco juice into his green can. "Now would be a mighty fine time to send that signal, Lieutenant."

"I'm with ya Tex." Sparkey held the transmit bar on his keyboard and tapped the send key. "And the signal is ... outta here," he said. All eyes turned toward Juan who sat with his headset over both ears now. His face was emotionless as he stared blankly at the floor, waiting for any indication that the satellite had accepted their coded message. Military activities in Egypt were difficult to monitor without detection. Miles and miles of flat open land made approach from the ground next to impossible. The simplest model radar unit could pick up a tin can tossed in the air eighty miles out. The super telephoto lens of a sophisticated satellite was the best bet for eavesdropping.

Sergeant Kennedy sat backward on his chair with his arms folded across the back. "What's the big deal?" he whispered. He was obviously bored. He kicked off with his right leg as if he were on a scooter and rolled over to Sparkey. "If we don't get it now, we can just catch it in a few hours when it comes around again, can't we?"

"Ordinarily yeah, but after going through these orders it

looks like they don't know how long these guys have been there and it seems they're expecting a bit of cloud cover that might screw things up for a day or two," Sparkey said, tapping his finger on a disk in his left hand. "By tomorrow the whole show could be over and we would never know what was goin' on ... at least not any time soon."

"Ya know what ah think?" Tex added as he gathered up another pinch from his tobacco pouch. "Ah think our intelligence boys got caught with their pants down. We shoulda known 'bout this mess long before now."

"Who knows?" Sparkey sighed and threw up both his arms. The chain on his left wrist rattled against the wall. "As long as we keep track of stuff comin' from all those satellites and keep everybody's little paws away from all these records, no one can say we're not doin' our job."

Sergeant Kennedy stood up, turned his chair around, sat back down and leaned back. "If people knew what some of those satellites were really capable of doing," he started, "they would ..."

"Lieutenant!" Juan interrupted. He sat up straight with his hands on each side of his headset. "Sir, do you know exactly what a Russian desert uniform looks like?"

"Well ... no ... not exactly." Sparkey looked puzzled from Tex to Sergeant Kennedy and back to Juan. "Why?"

"Cuz in a few minutes, sir, we can get you some fresh clear photos of the uniforms on the Russian troops in Egypt." Juan smiled. "She got the signal and is changing orbit! No problem!"

Throwing his headset on the keyboard, Juan jumped up, stomping his feet in a mock run. His hands held high over his head, palms out as he stomped toward Tex. "Ya-hoo" the big Texan yelped stomping in a similar fashion around the big glass map and toward Juan. "Stockford late shift has done it ah-gen! Group photos, courtesy of the most expensive photo lab in the world."

Like two football players just scoring a touchdown, Juan and Tex jumped high in the air, smacking their palms together in a well-deserved high-five. All of the men laughed as the two jokesters danced and celebrated their small victory in espionage photography.

Sparkey, still smiling, carefully copied some information into his orders manual, then counted the printed pages of data and code numbers he and his team had just used. Pulling the slack out of the chain leading to his wrist, he stretched around to a machine which slanted into a long one-inch wide slot near the top of the typewriter-sized unit. The tan shredder buzzed and vibrated as the documents labeled "Top Secret" now swirled into a wastebasket in the form of thousands of tiny white ribbons. The lieutenant turned back to his desk, quickly checked his notes and locked them in the safe beside him.

"Well now." Sparkey laced his fingers together across his chest and propped his feet on his desk. "Who wants to get the good lieutenant a diet cola? I'd get it myself," he added, "but, as you can see," he held up the chain, "I'm a bit tied up at the moment."

"I'm beginning to think you like being chained up over there," Sergeant Kennedy said, sliding his hand into his pocket to retrieve two quarters. "Anybody else?"

Sparkey smiled and handed the sergeant fifty cents. Tex peeled a dollar bill from a money clip. "I'll take an orange soda since you're goin' Sarge." He handed the bill to Kennedy. "Hope that changer's workin'."

"There's a trick to it," the sergeant said taking the bill from Tex. "First, you gotta make sure ..."

Bleep! ... Bleep! ... Bleeeeeep! ... Bleeep! The piercing blast of an alarm smothered Sergeant Kennedy's sentence.

"What the hell is that one?!" Sparkey jumped up. "That's not fire!"

Every man was on his feet. If the alarm was a fire alarm, there were certain procedures each person was to follow to protect documents and disks from damage. On the other hand, if this was an intrusion alarm those very same documents and disks would be intentionally destroyed.

Bleep! ... Bleep! ...

"Shit! If this is some kind of test," Sparkey reached for the black phone on the left, "I think we're flunking!"

"Wait a minute!" Corporal Beck said stepping into the doorway and looking down the hall. He turned and looked back into the control room at his lieutenant. "Sir, I think that's the intrusion alarm from somebody tripping the infrared beams."

Bleep! ... Bleep! ...

"This is Lieutenant Curtis. What's going on guys?" Sparkey listened to the dead line as he watched his team gather documents to be destroyed. Corporal Beck, Tex, Juan, Mark and Sergeant Kennedy all stood with stacks of papers and folders ready for the shredder.

"Come on people," Sparkey spoke into the silent phone. "We're gettin' ready to get rid of some important stuff here ... come on!"

Bleep!... Bleep!...

"Shit!" The now very frustrated lieutenant slammed the

receiver down on the phone. "Beck, hand your stuff over to Tex, run down the hall and see what the hell is going on. Get your weapon out ... and take off those stupid mouse ears, this still might be some kind of test."

The twenty-one-year-old technician nodded and handed an assortment of disks and electronic stat sheets to the big Texan.

"Ya want me ta go with 'im?" Tex asked Sparkey as he took the papers.

"Hang on everybody," Sparkey said, attempting to calm the group. "Beck, go ahead, check it out. None of us are supposed to leave this room in the first place!"

The corporal again nodded, clicking the safety off his .45 automatic. He rested his shoulder against the left side of the doorway. Holding the pistol firmly with both hands, Beck pointed the weapon towards the floor and peeked into the long hallway. Looking cautiously from left to right he eased out of sight.

Bleep! ... Bleep! ... The alarm continued, loud and irritating.

Sparkey and Tex stood looking at each other, nervously analyzing the events that were taking place. Beads of sweat were forming on the young lieutenant's forehead.

"All right Tex," Sparkey said finally, "go with him. I'm probably gonna get court-martialled for this anyway."

Tex moved around the corner of the large map toward Sergeant Kennedy. "Now don't you fret none, Lieutenant," Tex said, handing his double stack of papers to the older sergeant. "We'll find out what the hell is goin' on around this dat burn place."

"OK, listen!" Sparkey held up his right index finger. "You two go down the hall and look for the M.P. or the perimeter guards. If you don't see anything or anybody get your asses back here right away."

"No problem," Tex answered. He quickly spat his wad of tobacco into the green can and then pulled his heavy sidearm from its holster. Tex moved toward the door as he held the weapon to his side in his massive right hand. "Beck," he shouted stepping through the door into the noisy hall, "Hold on, I'm comin' with ya." He turned, winked at his worried lieutenant, then disappeared down the hallway.

What was becoming the longest minute in Lieutenant Curtis' career was being paced by the constant squeal of the intrusion alarm.

Blam!

The sound of a gun shot echoed from down the empty hallway.

Blam! Blam! Two more shots.

Sparkey grabbed the stack of classified bulletins and documents from his desk and tossed them into the shredder behind him.

"Zap 'em!" he shouted to the others as he pointed to their folders and then to the shredder.

Sergeant Kennedy moved over to the machine in time to see the last of the lieutenant's papers become confetti. The older sergeant dropped one of the three folders in his hand into the tray. Juan and Mark were soon by his side feeding their selected documents into the shredder.

Sparkey reached with his left hand and lifted the receiver of the second black phone from its cradle. "This is Lieutenant Curtis, clearance number three, seven, twenty-seven ... repeat ... three, seven, two, seven. We have a Code Four in "A" Building. This is not a drill. Shots have been fired ...   That's right, cut all power and seal the building!" Sparkey hung up the phone with his left hand while drawing his service automatic with his right. He looked at Juan, Mark and the sergeant standing with their guns ready, not pointed up in the air by their heads like in the movies, but down at the floor as they had been trained.

"Juan, get over by the door. Use the doorway for cover. Challenge anybody comin' down the hall and if they can't answer with the right word, blast 'em!" Sparkey ordered. His leadership abilities kicked into gear as he began to realize this was no test.

"Mark, move back to that far corner over there. Sarge, stay down between these two units. They should be shutting the power soon," Sparkey continued.

"The power?" Mark asked. He seemed a bit confused. "Sir, why cut the power?"

"Cuz," the lieutenant answered as he watched Juan peer down the hall, studying the radio man's face for any clues as to who the intruder might be. "No matter what, they can't force us to give up information from computers that don't have a power source, can they?"

There was a loud pop. The room fell dark and the hum of the various units faded. Control panels which seconds before were alive with hundreds of lights were now lifeless and black. The blaring of the alarm fell into a cold silence that was pleasant on the ears but uneasy on the nerves of the five men.

"I guess not, sir," Mark whispered a reply to his lieutenant's last question. He still was not sure of the advantages of not having any light just prior to confronting unknown intruders who were probably moving down the hall now if Beck and Tex didn't stop them.

There was a soft click as the emergency light came to life. The gray box was mounted high over the door with two spotlights on each side that illuminated a small area just inside the door of the control room. The battery-operated units didn't produce much light, but considering the circumstances, were greatly welcomed when compared with the several seconds of total darkness the nervous men had endured.

Everyone turned and looked at one another in the dim light and each gave a mental sigh of relief. Mark, however, gave his verbal approval of the light with "Geez! That's better!" and then wiped his sweaty palms on his pants. Juan inched toward the big door, crouched, his .45 felt weightless as the adrenaline raced through his body.

Slowly he again peeked down the long corridor. Emergency lights identical to the one over his head were spaced evenly down the hallway, creating small areas of light separated by larger areas of darkness.

"Can you see anything?" whispered Sparkey. Juan just shook his head slowly from side to side, straining his eyes to adjust to the dim light. After a few seconds he turned toward his lieutenant. "It looks like the emergency lights at the other end of the hall aren't working. It's all dark down there," he said, returning his attention back to the door.

Sparkey chewed his lowered lip while looking across into the dark corner at Mark, who was again wiping his palms. Sparkey then turned to the gray-haired sergeant just to his right. "What do you make of all this?" the young lieutenant whispered. "You've been around a lot longer than me. Any ideas?"

"I don't know, Sparks." Sergeant Kennedy moved his head slightly toward Lieutenant Curtis but kept his eyes trained on the door by Juan. "I've been thinkin' ... what do we have here that's worth all this to anyone? I mean ... the place is sealed outside by every swingin' dick at the base by now and we're right smack in the middle of the country. How do they expect to get outta here even if they get what they came for?!"

Sparkey started to answer but froze when he saw Juan suddenly tense up and point his pistol down the hall with both hands firmly around the grip. "Who's there?!" Juan shouted. "Tex ... Beck?!"

"What is it?!" the lieutenant asked. "Give the challenge!"

"Something!"

"Something my ass! Give the challenge!"

"I think it's just ..." Juan stepped a little further into the hallway.

"Keep covered!" Sergeant Kennedy shouted, but only too late.

Juan screamed a short loud scream. His gun clattered noisily to the floor. He staggered backwards through the doorway, slapping both hands to his throat as his second scream turned into a sickening gurgle. Thin jets of blood sprayed in all directions from between the doomed man's fingers.   Stumbling across test equipment Corporal Beck had been using, Juan fell crashing among many tools and computer parts, kicking and twitching in protest of his inevitable fate. The communication specialist became still. The grip he held on his own throat relaxed. Juan's life and blood were in a race to see which could leave his body the fastest. The growing pool of blood placed a close second as the younger soldier died.

"Jeez ... us!" Mark shouted. Flames a foot long leaped from the barrel of his .45 as he fired three shots through the dark doorway.

"Do you see 'em?!" Lieutenant Curtis shouted. He realized Mark was at a better angle to see who had attacked Juan.

"Jeez ... us!" the terrified soldier responded, staring at the doorway. It was obvious he was on the verge of firing more shots.

"What do you see man? Come on, answer me!" Sparkey shouted.

"I don't see shit!" Mark trembled as he aimed his gun at the same place he had just shot. "I don't see or hear shit, Lieutenant! What's goin' on?!"

"Hang on Mark ... just hang on! Don't shoot until you see what you're shootin' at. Beck or Tex might be coming through there."

"No sir!" Mark shook his head. "No sir! They aren't comin' back! ... I know they're not!"

"Now don't start crackin' up boy," Sergeant Kennedy spoke calmly to Mark. "We need you son, get a hold of yourself."

"I'm trying Sarge," Mark answered. He wiped his palms on his pants.

The sergeant looked slowly from Mark to the door, to the lieutenant, then his eyes locked in on Juan's body lying in a large scarlet puddle.

"Who would do all this, just for what we've got?" he muttered, bringing his weapon up and aiming at the entrance to their control room.

"Keep an eye on that door," Sparkey said as he reached for the red phone.

TWO

He casually held a .357 magnum to his right side in much the same way as an executive holds a briefcase. His stylish gray suit and charcoal dress hat were in total contrast to the rundown neighborhood in central Indianapolis known as "The Swamp." Michael Finder wished he had remembered to bring his sunglasses to block some of the bright afternoon sunlight that was beating down on him, in spite of his hat brim. A hot July breeze offered no relief as it blew Michael's unbuttoned jacket open, revealing a silver badge fastened to his belt.

The seventeen-year veteran stood six feet tall, not counting his hat, which he was almost never seen without. Some of his coworkers speculated that he even slept in that hat and often joked about how he kept it from getting wet in the shower. Black curly hair peeked out of all sides of the controversial headpiece that crowned his tanned, clean-shaven features. He was not at all "muscle bound," but was obviously in good shape, a result of five miles of running each morning and fairly controlled eating habits.

His job as a homicide detective often placed him in unnatural surroundings. Today was no exception. He was standing halfway up a flight of rickety, homemade stairs that ran up the outside of an old yellow two-story house that probably would have been condemned of it were located anywhere else but in The

Swamp. The upstairs of the house, in typical Swamp tradition, had been made into a separate apartment which had barely survived several generations of oversized families and undisciplined children. Two backyards over, a mange-infested brown mutt rummaged through the spilled contents of several trash cans.

Michael stood close to the house just under a window to the upstairs apartment. From there, he could not be seen from anyone inside. Occasionally, tattered white curtains would blow from the open window, popping softly over the detective's head. A baby was crying somewhere and in the distance, toward downtown, the wail of a siren echoed through the city. *Probably an ambulance*, Michael thought to himself as he squinted and looked up the stairs that led to the landing in front of the apartment door.

He had been up there twice before in the last month or so trying to catch up with a convicted murderer named Raul Martinez. Raul had gained front-page attention two years prior when he was sentenced to death for shooting a couple of convenience store employees. The bulky Puerto Rican from New York City had testified at his own trial that he "blew them away" because he enjoyed the feeling of power he got from ending a life. Pete Tucker, Raul's defense attorney at that time, sat with his face buried in his hands in total disbelief that his client would say such a stupid thing, even if it was true. It took the jury only twenty minutes to figure out an appropriate fate for Mr. Martinez and most of that time was used in walking to and from the courtroom.

A little more than a month ago, while on death row, Martinez broke the neck of a corrections officer and made a daring leap from a third-floor window of the city hospital. He had been awaiting treatment for a fake stomach problem that he had been setting up for quite some time.

At first, the most logical place for the killer to go was his ex-wife's apartment in the Swamp. After two visits they finally believed the ex-wife's story that Raul had gone to New York. After finding more pieces to the puzzle, Michael felt that Martinez had left the state at one time but was now back in town and most likely again in this apartment. After all, it had already been checked twice.

Standing three steps down from Michael was his partner, "Facts" as he was called by everyone including his wife. Facts had acquired his nickname in his pre-teen years because of his unique photographic memory. He remembered everything he ever read or heard. On slow days Facts would entertain the office by selecting a book of their choice from his enormous mental library; he would select a specific page and paragraph and begin reciting word-for-word to his amused audience. Although he was a straight-A student in high school and college, Facts had been completely bored with classes, having memorized all of his text and reference books.

Standing five feet nine inches tall and weighing in at just under two hundred pounds, it was obvious that this chunky officer was not the least bit interested in physical exercise. With his thinning brown hair and round thick glasses, Facts made a perfect thirty-two-year-old nerd.

In spite of any of Facts' shortcomings, Michael liked his partner. Although he felt that Facts wasn't exactly a great detective, the man's memory capabilities were fascinating and valuable.

"Well Michael?" Facts said impatiently. "If you think he's here, let's go get 'im. I'm getting hungry."

"Shhhhhh!" Michael whispered. "I kinda wanted this to be a surprise visit."

"Sorry. Forgive the shit outta me!"

"Let's give the district guys a little more time to get in place. I'm sure he's here this time."

"That's what you said the last time we were here."

"OK, so this time it's for real."

"Yeah? I think you're just checking out his ex, Maria."

"Get outta here," Michael said, almost embarrassed. He smiled and turned to look up the stairway again.

"Yo, Michael!" Facts tugged on the coattail of his partner standing a few steps above him. "I wouldn't blame you if you were coming back to check her out. Remember the last time we were here, June 21 at 11:06 ... remember Michael? She had on that skimpy little teddy thing that you could see right through."

"Yeah, yeah, I remember."

" ... And it pushed her boobs up so that they pointed kinda upwards with that deep cleavage and everything!"

"Yeah, OK, I remember, man." Michael interrupted Facts as he got louder the more he reflected back on their last visit with Maria.

"Sorry." The shorter officer smiled and reached into the right side of his waistband, drawing his snub-nose .38 revolver. He opened the cylinder, checked that it was loaded properly, then snapped it closed again.

"Yo, Michael."

"What?" came the irritated reply.

"I can't help thinkin' about you standin' there, starin' down at those tits, askin' the same questions over and over again. I've never seen you take so long to question anybody in my life."

Michael's face, which had been emotionless, suddenly broke into a smile. He forced his lips together as an uncontrolled chuckle hissed through his nostrils. Facts' whole body shook as he pressed his left hand against his mouth in an attempt to suppress the wave of laughter that had overtaken them.

"Was it that obvious?" Michael asked in a loud whisper as he regained control and wiped a tear from his eye with his free hand.

Facts, who was still losing it, was only able to nod his beet-red face up and down. He pinched his nose in a somewhat unsuccessful effort to stay quiet.

After a few seconds, both men had settled down and had regained their composure. "Oh, what the hell," Michael finally said in a normal tone of voice. "We couldn't have slipped up on Helen Keller with all of the noise we've been makin'."

He turned and started up the steps. "Come on, let's go get this clown."

"Yo, maybe we'll catch her in the shower this time," Facts speculated, eagerly bounding up the stairs behind his partner.

"Get outta here."

Michael climbed to the top of the stairs. He carefully stepped across the landing to the opposite side of the apartment entrance. Facts stopped just short of the landing on the first step.

Both detectives instinctively stood with their backs against the wall, careful to stay clear from the front of the door. Using the butt of his chrome magnum, Michael reached across to the center of the flimsy door and pounded out four hinge-shaking knocks that thundered through the neighborhood sending a nearby flock of birds into flight.

Silence was the only response to the officer's hammering. As he trained his ears for any sounds from the apartment, Michael's eyes wandered first from the weathered wood slats that they were standing on, to the gold ring on the chubby finger of his partner as he held his revolver with both hands in front of his round belly. It was about then that Michael first noticed a thick black cable hanging from the butt of Facts' gun. The cable or nylon cord, as it turned out to be, hung down just about two feet, then curled up and disappeared under the detective's suit jacket.

"What the hell is that?" Michael asked, straining his eyes to see better without moving from his position. Facts looked where he thought his friend was staring.

"Whataya think it is? It's a gun. It may not be a big shiny gun like yours, Professor Finder, but, nevertheless, it's still a gun," Facts answered sarcastically.

"No ... that black, stringy thing. What's that all about?"

"Ohhh that!" Facts realized what Michael was talking about. "That's my insurance policy," he said tugging firmly on the cord with his left hand. "I read the day before yesterday that 20 percent of all policemen that are killed on duty are shot with their own guns."

Michael gave one long, thoughtful nod.   "OK, I'm

listening," he said reaching across and knocking five more times on the apartment door.

"Well ... " Facts continued, "If I should ever drop my gun while wrestling with some dirtbag out here, instead of the dirtbag picking up my gun and smokin' me with it, I just give the ol' cord a yank, and lo an' behold my piece comes runnin' back to Daddy ...who then smokes the dirtbag." He smiled, proud of his little scenario.

"Ohhh-kay," Michael said doubtfully, while rolling his eyes and attention back to the situation at hand.

"Well, I thought it was a good idea," Facts said quietly and with a little mock disappointment.

"Oh ... it's a great idea! I just hope you never have to throw your gun to me in a pinch."

"Yo ... What makes you think I'd throw my gun to you anyway?"

"We would stand a better chance," Michael answered. "I've seen you shoot."

"Yeah? Well, after watchin' you catch this past season in softball, my best bet would be just to hang on to my gun an' pistol whip my way to safety."

The two policemen smiled at each other. Facts started to reach out and do some knocking of his own when they heard the soft thumps of footsteps approaching the door inside.

"Who's there?" a muffled female voice shouted. The heavy Spanish accent was obvious.

"Police, Maria! Open up!" Michael shouted with authority.

"What do you want this time?" came the voice with a

touch of anger. "I told you, Raul's not here. Leave me alone."

"Open ... the ... door, Maria!"

After a slight pause, the deadbolt clicked and several chains and sidelocks snapped and rattled. The door creaked as it slowly opened about three feet, partially exposing a pretty woman with smooth brown skin, black wavy hair and beautiful brown eyes.

Facts peeked around the edge of the door at Maria. She wore a pair of baggy tan shorts and an extra large Indianapolis Colts T-shirt that all but engulfed her petite frame. He turned away from her well-hidden figure with a tiny sigh. "So much for that," he mumbled.

"What'd you want?" Maria said, almost pouting. "Raul's not here."

"We're just going to take a quick look around," Michael said, cautiously pushing the door open further with his left hand.

Maria quickly placed both hands on the edge of the door, stopping it from opening any wider.

"Do you have a search warrant?" she asked.

"Oh, I don't believe this!" Michael said sounding upset. "We were getting along so well on our last two visits. This is definitely a personality change for you Maria ... Wouldn't you say, Facts?"

"Definitely," Facts nodded.

"How is it, my dear," Michael continued, "that before, when we came by, you let us look around. Now, all of a sudden, you're blockin' the door and asking about ... Wait a minute ... You're not hiding anything , are you? Facts, I think she's hiding something."

"Yeah, she is."

The two officers knew that Maria was not the type of person who was good at lying. She looked as if she were about to cry. With a quick, but unexpected move, the small woman tried to slam the wooden door shut. Simultaneously, Facts and Michael threw their shoulders into the door. Splinters and screws went in all directions as hinges ripped from the molding. The efforts of the detectives, especially the heavier Facts, buckled the door and sent it crashing across the kitchen. Maria, slid across worn tiles of the kitchen floor on her back.

Michael went in first, stepping across large pieces of wood and splinters that had once sealed the entrance to the apartment. He gripped his magnum revolver with both hands and pointed the large handgun toward the room next to the kitchen which, due to fewer windows, was slightly darker.

Facts stepped in close behind his partner, then moved to the left, staying against the wall. With his right hand, he pointed his .38 at the potential danger of the adjoining room. His left hand raised to caution Maria, who was starting to stand. "Don't move!" he shouted. "Just stay right there."

The teary-eyed Maria eased back down into a sitting position on the floor, using the cabinet doors under the sink as a back rest.

"Raul!" Michael shouted into the doorway ahead. "We know you're in here, man." He inched forward, staying close to the wall on his right. His eyes danced from left to right looking for any movement, any change, anything that would keep Detective Finder from going home this evening. "C'mon, man," he again shouted at the walls. "We don't want any trouble. You've got some dues to pay."

Michael had worked his way up to the right side of the

entrance into the next room. He peeked around into a large living room area for possible hiding places. With the exception of the buzz of a few flies and what was probably the hum of a fan somewhere down a hallway on the side of the living room, the place was quiet. Too quiet, Michael thought.

With his left hand he pointed to the hall that branched off to the left across from where he stood.

Facts cautiously eased across the kitchen past a small table and chairs, Maria and a plastic trash can that was long overdue for emptying. He took cover on a section of wall between a narrow utility closet and the entrance into the next room opposite Michael.

"Hear that?" Michael asked, nodding toward the corner of the hall.

"A fan, isn't it?" Facts said.

"Yeah. On a hot day like today, that's where I'd be."

"Yo, the way I see it, I'd be sprawled out on the bed in my underwear, right under that fan tryin' to cool off."

"Yep, I think you're right."

The end of the hall absorbed the detectives' full attention as Michael slid quietly into the next room. Maria said a short sentence in Spanish.

"Just be still," Facts cautioned her, without taking his eyes off of the hallway. If she was trying to distract him she would have to do better than that, he thought.

Slowly the door to the small utility closet behind Facts began to open.

It did not seem physically possible for the killer's huge frame to fit in such a small space. But still, like an evil cloud, he emerged from the closet into the kitchen.

Raul glanced at Maria who still sat on the floor. His eyes were dark and hateful. A gray bandanna crudely tied across his forehead held back some of the stringy black hair that hung below his shoulders. Workouts in the prison weight room had built a muscular chest and arms on an already dangerous man. He wore blue jeans and worn sneakers, but no shirt. His dark brown skin glistened with sweat as he turned from his steamy hiding place and started for the chubby, unsuspecting detective who had disturbed his afternoon.

As Raul moved in behind Facts, his large body blocked the sunlight that was shining through the broken kitchen door, casting a noticeable shadow.

Facts saw the shadow and turned just in time to catch a glimpse of a large brown fist just before it smashed into his face. Raul's powerful punch snapped the cartilage in Facts' nose and drove his upper teeth through his lip. Blood and the remains of the officer's glasses went everywhere. Stunned, Facts went crashing into the wall, then eased to the floor.

Michael lunged to defend his fallen partner. With all of his strength, aided by adrenaline, Michael savagely swung his heavy chrome revolver in an arc that started somewhere near the floor and ended across Raul Martinez's forehead knocking his bandanna to the floor. The felon slapped both hands to his head, bellowing a cry of pain.

More than once in his seventeen years of police work, Michael had used this technique to neutralize violent suspects. People that were struck in the head with his gun instantly became what some coppers jokingly called members of the Detective Finder Pistol Club. These new members were guaranteed a free and speedy trip to the local hospital.

Michael felt confident that Raul would soon be added to the list of new club members. He cautiously watched as Raul stood holding his head. One second ticked by, then another.

Slowly, the monstrous Raul pulled his hands from his head and angrily glared at the shocked detective. "You fucking pig! That hurt!!"

Michael had never before seen anyone remain standing, let alone talking, after having a heavy chrome .357 magnum bounce off his head.

"Ohhhhhhhh-kay," he said, bringing his revolver up and pointing it at the murderer. "I'm running out of options. The party's over. Turn around and put your hands behind your back or I'll replace that hickey on your head with a bullet hole."

Raul was like a cornered animal. He looked wildly to his right at Maria then sharply turned to the left and looked down at Facts. His frantic gaze then darted from Michael's eyes to the gun, then back again.

"Don't even try," Michael warned. "I'll blow you away. I swear I will!"

Reluctantly the enormous Martinez turned his back to the seasoned officer. Michael pulled his handcuffs from the waistband of his suit pants and carefully moved toward the man.

Facts, still stunned, his face covered with blood, had managed only to prop himself up on one elbow as he was still shaking some of the cobwebs loose.

Michael moved one more step closer. If he could just get handcuffs on this powder keg, he thought, this whole Raul Martinez fiasco would be over.

Raul's head ducked down and forward. Before Michael

could determine what exactly was happening, Raul had already thrown a powerful right leg backward, driving his dirty size twelve sneaker into the detective's midsection.

With a "whoosh" the air was stomped from the detective's lungs. Michael's charcoal gray dress hat toppled to the floor. He was literally kicked out from underneath it. Landing on his side with his knees up by his chest, Michael gasped desperately for air. His lungs would not follow the command to breathe. Like a drowning victim on dry land, Michael's face turned blue, his eyes bulged and his mouth gaped wide, but still, no air would enter his body.

Facts realized the seriousness of the situation and was summoning all of his power to try anything that might save him and his partner. Unable to stand, he slid his right hand along his belt, finding and gripping the nylon cord that was securely tied there. Both of Facts' eyes were swollen and, without glasses, anything more than a foot or two away was just a blur. As he pulled the cord he could barely make out a small dark mass sliding towards him through drying blood and broken glass.

"Come to Poppa," Facts mumbled to himself and pulled his .38 revolver closer.

Finally, air entered Michael's lungs. Not a lot of air, but after a few seconds of no air, a thimble-full would have been welcomed. He exhaled, then drew in another breath, larger than the one before. Odd, he thought, how when you're not breathing, no matter what's going on around you, you can't think about anything except breathing. For the first time since Michael had been kicked, he realized he was empty handed.

He quickly looked around taking inventory. His hat was sitting upright on the floor just below his feet. That wasn't what

Michael was looking for. Again, his eyes raced along the floor.

There! he thought, as he locked in on his gun a foot away beside the kitchen wall. He reached and eagerly curled his fingers around the butt of his chrome magnum. "Now," he said gathering his feet beneath him, "What's Martinez up to?"

Facts' idea with the cord on his gun had come through for him, but as soon as he reached to scoop up the weapon, the heel of Raul Martinez came crashing down on the officer's pudgy hand. Facts screamed as Raul picked up and settled the .38 into his giant palm.

"No way, Piggy," Raul's voice thundered as he continued to grind Facts' hand while eyeing his newfound toy.

"Say goodnight, asshole," Michael's angry voice came from behind Raul's right shoulder. He leveled his .357 at the huge felon.

Raul spun and pointed Facts' gun at Michael. It was now or never, Michael thought, as he squeezed back on the trigger preparing to end Martinez's life. At that same instant he caught a glimpse of Maria's small figure in the corner of his eye.

She came from nowhere, diving at him and slashing her fingernails across his face. She grabbed the sleeve of his gun arm, just as the weapon fired, sending the bullet off of its intended target, into a toaster across the room, spewing plastic and metal pieces to oblivion.

"Damn it!" Michael yanked his right arm and gun from Maria's grip. With his left arm he slammed her against the wall behind them. "Damn it, get back!" he shouted.

Maria bounced like a rubber ball off of the wall and back at Michael. This time she jumped on his back, her left hand across his eyes while her right hand clamped around the barrel of his gun, wrestling it in every direction except where the frustrated detective needed.

After several unsuccessful tries to free his hand from Raul's two hundred plus pounds, Facts strained his head upward and helplessly watched him point the .38 snub-nose at Michael's exposed chest.

Something dark and blurry was waving beside Facts' head. *The cord*! he thought, swinging his free left hand in an awkward hooking motion towards the blur. Two of his fingers caught the cord that ran from his belt to the gun in Raul's hand. Facts squeezed his fist around the strong nylon fibers and pulled with all of his might.

Raul fired just as the string hanging from the butt of the gun drew taut, pulling the shot down and to the left. The barrel belched a small flame as the bullet thumped into the plaster wall, narrowly missing Michael and Maria as they continued to struggle.

Raul, angered by Facts' interference, turned the sights of the gun at the portly policeman's head.

Facts had not prepared for this turn of events.

"Ohhhh ssshit!!" he hollered, as he wildly swung the nylon cord.

Raul fired, sending a shock wave across the entire kitchen floor as the bullet punched a neat hole in the tile less than an inch from Facts' head.

Raul fired again. Another hole popped into the floor, just on the opposite side.

Facts' frantic tugging was enough to keep the killer from hitting his mark. Raul was enraged. His knuckles cracked as he tightened his right hand on the grip of the gun. After wrapping two loops of the cord around his left hand, he brought both fists close to his chest and began to pull. Raul clenched his teeth as every muscle in his powerful shoulders and neck rippled to life.

Sounding like a tiny firecracker, the nylon cable snapped under the tremendous strength of the felon's mighty arms. Raul unwrapped the loose cord from his left hand and casually tossed it on top of Facts, who still clutched his end of the string as if, somehow, it would make a difference.

"Looks like you're at the end of your rope, fat boy," Raul said coldly down at Facts.

The battle between Michael and Maria raged on. After pulling his gun hand from Maria, for what seemed like the hundredth time, Michael balled his fist and sent a hard left hook crashing into the tiny girl's jaw. The punch put her down and out for the count.

Having heard the shots in the other corner of the room, Michael feared his partner was already dead. He spun to do what he had been trying to do for the last few seconds ... shoot Raul.

As Michael brought his gun up and around, he was already applying pressure on the trigger. To Michael's surprise, Raul was much closer than expected. Instead of the killer hovering over Facts, as he was seconds before, Raul was now less than a foot from the end of Michael's revolver. In that short moment of confusion Michael froze. His hesitation cost him what was probably his last chance of survival.

Raul drove his left forearm up and out, catching the startled cop's arm and gun, pinning them to the wall. His right hand brought Facts' .38 up into the soft part of Michael's throat under the chin.

"Drop it!" he snarled, shoving the barrel of the gun deeper into the officer's flesh.

Michael's mind raced, searching for any alternative to dropping his weapon. Realizing time was not on his side, he reluctantly opened his fingers and the chrome magnum fell to the floor with a loud clunk.

Raul grabbed Michael by his tie and pulled him out from the kitchen wall, shoving him more into the open.

"I could've killed you easy, man," Raul threatened.

"Why didn't you?"

"Why?" The convict flared and stepped directly in front of Michael. "Because we have something to settle."

Their eyes met in a cold, emotionless stare. Michael remembered Raul's reputation for humiliating his victims before he brutally killed them.

A smile broke across the murderer's face as he playfully patted the detective on the cheek. Without warning he flipped his right arm back, sending the pistol crashing into the top of Michael's head.

"That, Dog, is for putting your hands on me," Raul said.

The force of the blow knocked Michael to his knees. Pain shot through his head like lightning as a mixture of sweat and blood oozed down the left side of his face. Kneeling on all fours, red droplets stained the floor and Michael's gray hat as it lay where it had fallen earlier. Looking around, his vision went double, then triple, and back to double again.

Don't pass out, Michael thought to himself, *Just hang on*

... Hang in there, he kept mentally repeating.

"Get up!" Raul commanded. "I'm not through with you. Get ... up!"

Michael collected himself on unsteady legs and slowly rose to face Raul once more. He had retrieved his hat and was holding it with both hands at about waist level. The top of the hat, complete with fresh bloodstains, faced Raul.

The killer pointed. "What is this?" he teased. "Your good luck charm?"

"Apparently not," Michael said softly. He nervously rotated his headdress while the fingers on his right hand searched the inside of the brim. He calmly looked into the convict's eyes.

Slowly, Michael located and unsnapped a hidden pouch inside the hat. A tiny pearl-handed derringer, not bigger than a cigarette lighter, slid from the pouch into Michael's palm.

"You got anything to say?" Raul asked as he cocked the gun and held it to the officer's head. "Something short will do."

Michael said nothing, but moved his hat over to the left revealing the little two-shot gun, pointed upward at a forty-five degree angle between them.

It was Raul's turn for surprise. His eyes widened when he realized what his intended victim had literally pulled from his hat.

The small weapon popped like a cap gun as Michael squeezed the trigger. Raul's head rocked backwards, then slowly came forward. His face went totally blank and his arms went relaxed to his sides.

A single scarlet dot appeared in the center of Raul Martinez's forehead. One drop of blood formed and ran down the side of the killer's nose, over his lips and around the curve of his chin. Other drops quickly followed, creating a steady stream that began to splatter at his feet. Facts' .38 that Raul had been holding clattered noisily to the tile floor.

"Asshole," Michael said.

Raul's eyes rolled back and, like a fallen timber, he went crashing to the floor. The state's promise of death had been fulfilled.

Michael ran and knelt by his partner's side. He let out a sigh of relief when he saw Facts bring his hands to his head and moan.

"Thank God," Michael said, then turned and sat on the floor.

Facts strained to look at his friend through two swollen eyes.

"Martinez?" he asked.

"Dead, I hope," Michael answered.

"You OK?"

"Yeah, I'm all right."

"You hungry?"

"Get outta here."

THREE

"Holy Sweet Jesus!" Colonel Freedman said, looking down on the bodies of the two guards that were stationed outside "A" Building.

Their throats had been cut almost completely through. A few feet away lay the blood-soaked carcasses of three attack dogs.

The colonel turned to a sergeant standing behind him. "Any word from Lieutenant Curtis, or the other men inside?" he asked.

"No sir, not a word."

"Do you think there's a chance that whoever did this is still in there, Sergeant?"

"Hard to say, sir ... There's a report of a hole in the wall on the north side, at ground level, but we've got the building surrounded."

"Is our entry team ready?"

"Yes sir. Twelve men sir!"

"OK," the gray-haired colonel said, turning back to face the eerie darkness of the building. "Turn the power back on and unseal the doors. Let's find out what in the hell is going on."

"Yes sir."

" ... And Sergeant," the colonel added, " ... If you can take someone alive ... well ... we'll probably have a lot of questions for them."

"I understand sir."

The sergeant moved toward a group of fatigue-clad soldiers kneeling in the early morning darkness.

After a few minutes, the overhead lights flickered to life in the hallways and offices of "A" Building. Half of the assault team, led by Colonel Freedman, filed through the unsealed main door crouching behind the front desk for cover. Seconds later, the other half followed the sergeant through the same door.

The grisly scene that met the soldiers just inside the entrance turned even the strongest stomachs. Slouched in a chair at the security station sat the headless, bloody body of the M.P. Blood stained the wall from the floor to the ceiling behind the corpse.

Colonel Freedman peeked down the long corridor from over the top of the security desk. One third of the way down the hall, in a large pool of crimson gel, lay two more lifeless forms.

"Who are we dealing with here?" the colonel quietly asked himself.

He looked back at the faces of the men behind him. There were expressions ranging from anger to fear. A young private immediately behind Colonel Freedman stared blankly at the carnage in the brightly lit hallway. His face was pale as milk.

"Are you all right son?" the colonel asked.

The private merely nodded his head up and down.

"You're not lookin' too good."

Again the soldier nodded.

"Sergeant!" the colonel called out.

Instantly, the rugged team leader was at the colonel's side. "Sir?"

"I'm not sure what we're dealing with here," Colonel Freedman said. "Terrorists maybe ... a group of psychos ... who knows?"

"Colonel, I think that with the aggressive nature of these attacks, whoever did this would have probably attacked us by now if they were still here."

"I agree," the elderly officer said as he stood. "Men, check the other rooms, and don't move any bodies unless you have to. Besides, there's nothing you can do for these poor souls anyway."

As the soldiers carefully made their way down the hall, Colonel Freedman looked at the team leader beside him. "The sergeant and I will check the control room," he said loud enough for the others to hear.

As they started in behind the troops, the colonel suddenly hesitated. "Oh," he said turning to find the pale-faced eighteen-year-old he had talked to earlier, "Private!"

"Sir?" came the meek reply.

"We need one man posted just outside the door to keep watch over the crime scene. Can you take care of that for me?"

"Yes sir." The young boy tried to smile in spite of his churning stomach. "Thank you sir." He turned and darted into the fresh air.

The sergeant and Colonel Freedman holstered their weapons as they stood looking down at Juan's body grotesquely draped among the many meters, probes, and tools to the left of the control room entrance. His throat and eyes gaped open.

"Juan Santinos," the colonel said shaking his head. "A good kid. A real good kid." He looked up and walked across the bloodstained floor into a second aisle past a huge glass map. To his left, at the opposite end of the map, a severed hand lay in a reddish brown puddle of partially dried blood. The fingers of the hand still curled loosely around the butt of a service weapon. In the background, Mark lay dead – face down in his own gore.

"Colonel! Quick! Over here!" the sergeant yelled. "It's Sergeant Kennedy. He's been shot but I think he's alive."

"Carl?" Colonel Freedman knelt beside Kennedy, who was lying between two computer consoles. "I didn't know he was working. Get a medic. Hurry!"

The team sergeant nodded and left the room without a word.

"John?" Sergeant Kennedy said, looking up at the colonel.

"Yes ... Yes ... Help is on the way."

"John." Kennedy's voice was weak. "John ... it was ..."

"Who was it Carl? Who were they?"

"Just ... one ..."

"Medics on the way, Colonel!" a voice shouted from the door.

Colonel Freedman ignored the information and leaned closer to the fallen sergeant. "Just one what, Carl?" he asked. "What do you mean?"

"Just ... one ... did all ... this."

"You can't mean that. How?"

"Fast... John ..." Kennedy's voice began to trail off. "I've ... never ... seen ... anybody move like ... that."

"Did you recognize anything, Carl? A uniform? A patch maybe?"

Sergeant Kennedy's grip relaxed on Colonel Freedman's arm. He was barely able to whisper his last words. "Sorry, John," he said. Then his eyes closed for the last time.

John Freedman slowly stood. "Too late," he quietly said to the med techs that had just raced into the room. The team sergeant stood silently by the commanding officer's desk area and nodded towards a body on the floor.

"Is it Lieutenant Curtis?" the colonel asked.

"Yes sir."

Colonel Freedman looked at the young lieutenant's body and sighed. "Sparkey," he said.

"And sir," the sergeant pointed to the empty strong box beside the desk, "they got the code disks and orders manuals."

"Why would anyone go through all this trouble just for our codes?" the colonel thought out loud.

He turned to leave the control room with its ill-fated crew. His eyes froze momentarily on the chain beside the command desk. Hanging from the end of the chain was the severed hand of the lieutenant.

"Sweet Jesus!" the colonel said. "I'm closing down every inch of this place."

Colonel Freedman stepped back into the hallway with the sergeant at his side.

One of the assault team soldiers ran up to the two men. "Sir," he said, "the building checks are clear. It looks like they got out through that hole in the wall in the dish maintenance room."

"We'll find out who did this," the colonel said. "Get me Major Hamilton."

FOUR

"I felt like saying 'Of course killing him was necessary, otherwise I wouldn't have shot him in the head, numb-nuts!'" Michael said to Facts as they briskly walked from police headquarters. A lunchtime crowd was enjoying the sun and cuisine at the City Market across the street.

"Yeah, I hate the Firearms Review Board too. Those guys act like they were never on the streets."

"That Captain Sweeny," Michael continued, "asked me why I didn't have my mace – of all things!"

"What did he want you to do, spray Martinez between shots?" Facts asked.

"I don't know what he wanted, but I tell ya, that's why I never want to be promoted. I'd wear this silver badge fifty more years before I'd become some kind of paper-pushin' puppet inside. I like the streets. You can just go after bad guys and not worry about all the bureaucratic... " Michael's sentence trailed off as he noticed he was talking to himself. His partner was nowhere to be found.

"Yo, Michael!" Facts' voice came from down the sidewalk. He was standing next to a hot dog vendor that had set off his snack-time alarm clock. "Yo! Ya want one of these?" he asked. "They're great."

"Aw man!" Michael scrunched up his nose. "You don't need that junk. Let's go get a salad or something."

"No. This is great. Really!" Facts was squeezing a trail of mustard along the length of a jumbo frank that had already been smothered with chili sauce and onions.

"Anyway," he added as an afterthought, "I've been cutting down."

"Cutting down?" Michael laughed. He reached over and patted his partner's round gut. "On what? The world hot dog supply?"

"Only a communist wouldn't eat a hot dog," Facts said, leaning over to take a bite.

"Come on," Michael said.

The two men turned and continued in their original direction down the sidewalk.

"Control, 47-57." The dispatcher's voice blared from the radio clipped to Michael's belt.

Michael brought the radio to his lips and pressed the black button on the side.

"47-57, go ahead control," he said.

"Sir, Adam Sector marked units are calling for a homicide detective at 1200 West 38th Street."

"What have they got there ma'am?"

"Sir, I believe two bodies. Adam 34 said he'd explain more when you were there."

"I'm clear."

"Thank you sir."

"Nothing like two stiffs on a warm summer morning to get the ol' blood going, huh?" Facts said, tearing another bite from his hot dog.

"Yeah, just great." Michael wasn't the least bit enthusiastic. "What's at 1200 West 38th Street?"

"That's the Indianapolis Museum of Art," Facts said, catching a drip of chili sauce in his napkin. "I've been there. Nice place."

"I wonder what this is all about," Michael said. "You coming by?"

"Yeah, you go ahead. I've got to find something to wash this dog down with," Facts answered. "I'll be over in a bit."

The Indianapolis Museum of Art was a striking building built in the early 1970s. For as long as anyone could remember it had housed some of the finest works of art and artifacts from all over the world. Located near the heart of Indianapolis, the museum itself was a work of art and was proudly supported by the community.

Michael pulled beside one of three marked police cars in the museum's circular drive. As he got out of his car he felt the mist from the large landmark fountain in the center of the circle. A small group of reporters stood outside a bright yellow strip of crime scene tape that stretched across the entrance. Michael ducked under the tape and climbed the stone steps to the main doors.

"Hey, Jerry," he said to the uniformed policeman standing by the door.

"How ya doin' Michael?" The officer smiled and held the big glass door open for the detective. "You've got a good one."

"Great," Michael said. He walked through the door onto the carpeted lobby floor.

Another uniformed policeman was standing in the lobby busily writing in a small notebook. He looked up when Michael approached. "Are you Detective Finder?" he asked.

"Yep ... That's me."

"Third floor, sir," the officer said, pointing to the elevators with his ink pen. "The sergeant's up there with the crime lab."

"Thanks."

"Oh ... Detective Finder," the officer called out.

Michael hesitated as the elevator door opened and turned back toward the policeman. "Yeah?" he said.

"I hope you haven't had lunch, sir ... it's a good one."

"Thanks, I've been warned."   Michael turned and disappeared in the elevator.

Thirty-five-millimeter cameras whirred and flashed throughout the third floor as the crime lab technicians snapped pictures from every possible angle.

"Man o' man!" Michael said, looking down at the blood-covered floor in a display area on the third level.

One of the technicians was carefully straddling a pool of blood while he focused his camera lens on a hand lying by itself, palm up. Just to the side of the severed hand was a blood-smeared .38 caliber revolver. The camera flashed and the automatic film advance wound the film to the next frame.

"What-a-ya say, Michael?" the barrel-chested technician asked without looking up. He found another angle and snapped off another picture. The body of a man in a security guard uniform was lying face down near the middle of the splattered room.

"Is that *his* hand?" Michael asked, pointing to the corpse.

"Yeah ... I guess so ... he's missing one."

"Where's his head?"

"Over in the corner there." The technician nodded towards a hair-covered ball on the opposite side of the room.

Michael tilted his freshly-cleaned hat back and knelt beside a second corpse. This one was a man in his late fifties or early sixties. "Nice suit," Michael said, gently lifting one side of the dead man's jacket to examine a gaping bullet hole in the chest of the unfortunate victim.

"Well if it isn't Michael Finder," a silver-haired police sergeant said in a hearty voice. His hair was in a crewcut, and he chewed on an unlit cigar. "A pretty good one, huh?"

"That's what I hear," Michael said looking up. "How ya doin' Topper?"

"Couldn't be better."

"What've you got for me?"

"Well," the police sergeant started, "there are some things missing from crates in the other room over there. We don't know exactly what, but we're trying to get hold of a secretary. She might be able to help us with that." The sergeant thought for a second then pointed down at the body sprawled in front of Michael. "That," he said, "is Clevous Tiller, the director of the museum or something like that. We're checking with Grey Stone Security for an ID on the guard."

"You think the two of them stumbled across some bad-ass burglars?" Michael asked.

"Looks that way."

Michael turned to the crime lab technician. "Bobby, when you get done here I need the gun and the hand taken to the lab. I want to find out if the gun's been fired, and if that's the hand that fired it. Also be sure to get some good pictures of those footprints in the blood. We'll need a size on those if possible."

"You got it, Michael."

"Topper," Michael said. "Who found this mess?"

The sergeant flipped through some pages in his notebook. "Here we go," he said, holding his notes so Michael could see. "Roseanne Peaks from the cleaning crew. She's downstairs now ... pretty shook up I guess. She won't be much good for questioning right now."

"I imagine not," Michael said as he stood and surveyed the area again. "It's not every day a cleaning lady runs across a couple of chopped-up guys in an art museum." He walked to the doorway leading to the next room from which Topper had first emerged. "This is where the crates are?"

"Yeah, over to your left."

Michael and the sergeant were standing in a large room stacked to the ceiling with all kinds of containers and cases. A small wooden box was lying on its side, empty, at the base of a mountain of undisturbed crates. Beside the empty box was a six-foot-long glass display case. The glass doors in front were shattered. Only a base of some kind sat on the single shelf.

"Chinese," Michael said curiously. "Everything printed on these crates is in Chinese."

"Yeah," Topper said, "All sorts of art stuff probably."

"Well, they either knew exactly what this thing was packed

in and where it was stored, or they can read Chinese."

"That's true," Topper said, pulling the cigar from his teeth. "There's no way they could have found what they were looking for in all of these crates by just guessing."

"It's not very likely," Michael said thoughtfully. He lifted his hat up, fanned himself a few times, then carefully set his hat securely back on his head.

"Yo, Michael!" Facts called from the room where the bodies were. "You in there?"

Michael and the police sergeant walked into the room where the chubby detective stood, looking bewildered.

"What a mess!" Facts said. "Whatever happened to the good ol' days? ... Whatever happened to poison ... and strangulation? This," he gestured towards the head in the corner, " ... this ... is just down right tacky. Ya got any ideas yet?"

"No, not really," Michael said. "Maybe burglary ... there are some things missing from the other room ... Chinese stuff I think."

"Chinese?" Facts said. He looked puzzled for a second, then his eyes widened from excitement. "Yo! ... Not Chinese ... I bet it's Japanese! I read in last Sunday's paper, in the entertainment section, page five, about a rich Japanese guy's art collection on display here. Masato Kudo ... That's his name. It's supposed to be the largest private collection of ancient Japanese art in the world."

"OK," Michael said. "I still can't read it, but I think our murder suspects can. What else can you remember about the art show?"

"Well ..." Facts closed his eyes and began scanning the

newspaper article perfectly preserved in his memory. "It goes on to say ... Kudo has never publicly displayed his collection before and doesn't ever plan to do it again. He's been all over the United States, ending here ... in Indianapolis."

"Any particular work of art that would be worth killing over?" Michael asked.

"It doesn't say. Ya want me to recite the article to you ... it's about a quarter page."

"No, don't do that. Is there anything else of importance?"

"No, just that the show ended two days ago."

"That would make sense," Michael said. "They were probably packing everything for the return to Japan."

"Yeah, they were," Facts said snapping his fingers as he remembered something. "As a matter-of-fact, there's a great-looking lady downstairs, named Bonita Baker, that has something to do with this whole Japanese art show. Her name was in the office on a list of people to notify in case of emergency. I told her to wait downstairs ... thought maybe you would want to talk to her."

"That's great, Facts. She can probably help come up with whatever is missing from that box and display case. I'd better get down there now."

"Michael, she is a knock-out. I'll go with you an ... aw shit! What did I just step in?" Facts leaned against a wall and lifted his right shoe to look at the sole. "Shit!" he said again. "I've got some goo or something on my new shoes."

"It's gonna wear off by the end of today," Michael said.

"Great! I get to walk around all day with part of a dead guy on the bottom of my foot."

"I'm going down to talk to this Bonita Baker."

"Is there anyplace that washes the bottoms of shoes while-you-wait?"

"Are you gonna help me on this one?"

"Yeah, I'm coming ... I bet I'll be the only homicide detective in town with free samples on his shoe."

"Get outta here," Michael said, guiding Facts toward the elevators.

FIVE

Michael had never seen anyone like her in his life. Facts had made a serious understatement when he said Bonita Baker was a knock-out.

She stood in the museum office dabbing her emerald-green eyes with a lace-trimmed handkerchief. Her blond hair was pulled atop her head in a neatly woven braid. A slightly upturned nose and full lips enhanced her fashion-model face. Michael guessed her to be about five feet, eight inches tall. Most of her eye-catching figure consisted of a set of gorgeous legs that were visible beneath a knee-length white cotton skirt. A crisp white suit jacket with padded shoulders completed her very appropriate business attire.

"Bonita Baker?" Michael asked as he entered the office.

"Yes?"

"I'm Detective Finder. I'm a homicide detective for I.P.D."

The young woman nodded once. The concern was obvious on her face. "Who's been murdered? They won't tell me who it is," she said.

"I apologize," Michael said, motioning towards two office chairs. He paused while they both sat and adjusted the seats facing each other. "It's Mr. Tiller."

"Oh my God!" Bonita gasped. Her hands raced to cover

her open mouth. "My God!" she said again. "Why ... what happened?"

"All we know is that a lady on the cleaning crew found the bodies of Mr. Tiller and the security guard this morning."

"The guard too?"

"Yes ... I'm afraid so." Michael was trying to sound compassionate, but after seeing as many dead people as he had over the years, it was difficult to get emotional.

His nostrils were lightly teased with a faint whiff of her wonderfully sweet perfume. "I'm going to have to ask you some questions," Michael said. "Will that be all right?"

"Sure ... anything," she said sitting up straighter in her chair.

"How well did you know Mr. Tiller?" Michael asked. He flipped his notebook to a clean page and removed a pen from the inside pocket of his suit jacket.

"Not very well I guess," Bonita answered. "Just around here at work."

"When I saw you crying, I thought you may have already known."

"No ... I'm just upset about this whole thing. I've never had anything like this happen before."

"I understand," Michael said. "What exactly do you do here, Miss Baker?"

"Well ... I'm not really an employee of the museum. I've been hired by Mr. Kudo, the owner of the Japanese art collection ... We just ended our last showing here."

"That's what I hear. Go on."

"I travel with the show. We've been all over the United States. I'm responsible for every piece ... packing, shipping, and displays at all of the museums."

"That's a pretty neat deal," Michael said smiling. "How did you get this job?"

"Lucky, I guess," Bonita smiled back. "Plus, I was the most qualified for the job. I've spent several years going back and forth to Japan studying art and art history."

"Japan?" Michael asked. "You lived in Japan?"

"Yes, off and on ... What's so strange about that?"

"Well don't you have any family or ... anything?"

"Anything?"

"Yeah ... well ... you know," Michael began to stumble over his words, "a husband ... or boyfriend ... or big brother?"

Bonita giggled softly. "No, none of those. My parents died when I was very young."

"Oh, I'm sorry."

"There's nothing to be sorry about."

Michael shrugged his shoulders and nodded. He looked down at his notes briefly and tapped his pen a few times on his chin. "By any chance can you read Japanese?"

"Yes... Some," Bonita said. "I can understand the spoken language and I can speak it pretty well, but the Japanese use a lot of Chinese Kanji in their written language. I find that to be very confusing, but I guess I can hold my own."

Facts stepped through the doorway carrying the small box that had been lying on the floor in the storage room next to the bodies. "Yo, Michael. They're through with this, and I thought you might want to check it out before they took it downtown," he said.

"Yeah ... great," Michael said taking the case from his partner and turning the Japanese characters towards Bonita. "Do you know what was in here?" he asked.

She studied the box for a moment. "Oh no! That's the jade Haiku Dragon. Is it missing?"

"Yes. What about a glass display case that's beside all of the crates upstairs?"

Bonita's eyes widened. "That's a two-hundred-year-old samurai sword. Mr. Kudo will be sick. It was his favorite."

Michael looked up at Facts. "You know what I'm thinking?" Michael said.

"I have some idea," Facts glanced at Bonita then back at Michael and winked.

"I mean about this!" Michael said curtly.

"I give up, what do you think about this?" Facts asked.

"The murder weapon," Michael said. "... Don't you see?"

Bonita Baker didn't see. "What are you talking about?" she asked.

Michael realized he hadn't explained all of the details to her. "I suppose I can tell you," he said. "There was a ... well ... a decapitation."

"Oh no!" Bonita yelled. "You mean somebody's head was cut off upstairs?" As the picture in her mind developed of what a person would look like without a head, Bonita's complexion began to change to match her green eyes. She coughed unexpectedly, then gagged. Slapping her hand across her mouth, she hastily jumped from the chair, pushed Facts out of the way, and darted out the door toward the ladies' room.

"Way to go, you smooth talker you," Facts said, patting Michael on the back. "You certainly have a way with the women."

"I didn't mean to make her puke," Michael said. "I just think she can help us out on this."

"Now I understand why women come out of your office saying, 'That Michael Finder makes me sick!'" he said, his voice raised to a high, whiny pitch.

Both policemen chuckled quietly for a few seconds but were careful not to offend any of the more-concerned employees that may be in listening range.

"Isn't she beautiful?" Michael said, peeking at the door to make sure no one was there.

"Listen to 'im," Facts said. "It's amazing how your dick can talk and make your mouth move like that."

"Get outta here!"

"Well, before you run out to buy a station wagon, tell me what you think about this deal here today."

"Well," Michael started, "we've got somebody who can recognize the value of certain ancient Japanese art pieces. We have someone who probably can read Japanese, and we have a person who chose a samurai sword to take on an armed guard. That sounds like confidence to me, and well-deserved."

"I'll say. They sure knew what they were doing."

"I imagine we're looking for a Japanese guy who might have a hard-on for this owner-guy ... What's his name?"

"Masato Kudo," Facts said. "He's supposed to be one of

the wealthiest men in Japan."

"Yeah, Kudo. Well that would qualify him to have several enemies, probably," Michael said.

Bonita Baker stepped into the room looking somewhat embarrassed. "I'm so sorry," she said. "I just pictured that ... that... "

"No, I'm sorry," Michael interrupted. "I should have never sprung that on you like that."

"That's OK."

"Do you still feel like answering questions?"

"Yes, please go ahead."

"Did Mr. Kudo ever have any trouble with anybody during his tour of the United States?"

"No, not that I know of," Bonita answered thoughtfully.

"No threats or arguments?"

"No."

"How about in Japan, before the tour?"

"I don't think so. I seldom talked to Mr. Kudo directly. Japanese men are still a little backwards when it comes to dealing with women in business. I've talked to him on the phone, but I've never met him face-to-face."

Michael looked astonished. "You mean you've worked for him all this time, handling all of his valuable belongings, and you've never met the man?"

"Not really," Bonita said, looking from Michael to Facts. "It's part of his culture. Mr. Kudo is just a little set in his ways. In Japan he's done a lot of nice things for the Japanese people."

"Why are you working for him if he's like that?" Facts

asked sitting back on the edge of a desk.

"Well ... " she continued, "he pays well. It's work I enjoy doing. And besides ... I've seen more cities in America than most Americans have."

"I can see your point," Facts said. "Traveling all around and getting paid for it. I'd do it myself, but I have strict orders not to leave Michael unattended."

Bonita laughed and looked at the smiling Detective Finder. Michael simply shook his head from side to side and slid his hat backwards with the end of his pen. "This used to be a friend of mine," Michael said pointing a thumb at his partner.

"Don't listen to him," Facts cautioned. "He's never had any friends."

Bonita smiled, amused by the two men's jabs.

The smile on Michael's face slowly faded as his thoughts returned to the grisly scene two floors above. His dark eyebrows dipped slightly into a frown as he quickly analyzed different possibilities for a motive.

"What about ex-employees?" Michael threw the question out almost more as an idea than an actual question. "Any employees get fired or quit over in Japan before the art tour?"

"I don't think so. Mr. Kudo's art collection is pretty much a hobby. Most of his employees were part-time."

"Does he have any partners?"

"Uh ... yes!" Bonita's green eyes sparkled as she remembered an important point. "Not now, but before I started working for Mr. Kudo, he had a partner. A Mr. ... Mr. ... Tanaka ... That's it, Sumio Tanaka."

"What happened with this Tanaka?"

"Wait a minute ... He's here!"

"You mean here in America?"

"Well, yes. But I meant here in Indianapolis. I think he lives here."

"Oh get outta here!" Michael said, throwing his pen down on his notepad.

"No really!" Bonita looked desperately from one detective to the other. "I don't know if he still lives here, but the way I understand it ... he and Mr. Kudo each had their own collections. They grew up together or something like that and decided to combine their artifacts and started the shop in Japan where this collection came from."

"I'm listening, go on."

"Well ... apparently this Mr. Tanaka and Mr. Kudo got into some kind of disagreement. Mr. Tanaka sold his share of the shop to Mr. Kudo for the equivalent of just under two million dollars. He was paid in two checks. One right away, and the other one, an adjusted check, was mailed to the states, to an Indianapolis address. I saw a copy of it myself. No offense, but I remember thinking, of all places, why would he pick Indianapolis? I never gave it another thought until now."

"How do you know all of this?"

"When I realized I wasn't going to talk to Mr. Kudo very much, I was curious, so ... I asked. The Japanese like to gossip as much as anybody else, and besides, I'm nosy."

Michael smiled. "I like you." He picked up his pen, again pushed his hat back, and looked up. "Well Facts, have you ever read the phone book?" he asked.

Facts stood up, staring off into space, then closed his eyes.

He slowly rubbed his face with both hands and said nothing.

Bonita, her pretty face filled with concern, leaned in her chair trying to see Facts' face. "Are you all right?"

"Shhh!" Michael cautioned, bringing his finger to his lips.

"Is he ...?"

"Shhhh!"

"What's he ...?"

"SSHHHH!"

With his eyes still closed, Facts stood upright and snapped his fingers. "I'll be damned!" he said. "Here he is, Tanaka ... Sumio. On North Meridian Street." He recited the phone number.

Michael quickly scribbled the information on his pad. "Excellent!" he said, heavily dotting an "I."

"You remember that from reading a phone book?" Bonita Baker asked, somewhat bewildered.

Facts just nodded rapidly up and down with a cartoon smile.

"I am very impressed," she said, sitting back in her seat.

"I try," Facts said, proud of his feat. "I believe I'll go see what I can dig up on this Tanaka character, and maybe good ol' Mr. Kudo."

"That'll be good," Michael said. "I think I'll pay a little visit to the Tanaka household."

Facts shook the lady's hand and gave his friend a two-finger salute, then stepped out of the door.

"Why don't you go with me?" Michael asked Bonita.

"What do you need me for?"

"Well ... you know about Kudo, and the art stuff. He may be intimidated by you, knowing you've lived in Japan. That would make him less likely to try an' pull anything over on me."

"Do you always take civilians you've just met to interview suspects, Detective?"

"Yes, every time. I wouldn't be caught at an interview without a stranger," Michael said. "Of course ... the strangers always make me take them to lunch afterwards."

"What makes you think I'll be any different?"

"I was hoping you wouldn't be."

"I won't."

SIX

Going to visit a murder suspect that may have just chopped up a couple of people must have made Bonita Baker a little too uncomfortable. She convinced Michael to drop her off at a flower shop while he went alone to talk to Sumio Tanaka. The lovely art advisor had only agreed to go along for the promised lunch afterwards.

Besides, Michael had not really intended for Bonita to accompany him to Tanaka's house. It was just an excuse to take her out. He was glad she thought of getting flowers for her slain coworker's family. Honestly, the interview would go smoother without her.

His unmarked tan police car made its way up the suspect's long driveway that bordered almost an acre of immaculately landscaped grounds. After parking the car and scaling a series of stone steps, Michael swung the heavy brass knocker that centered an eight-foot by six-foot solid oak door. It was only then that he noticed a door bell off to the right and pushed it briefly.

He stepped a few steps away from the door to re-button the top button on his shirt and tighten his tie. *Nice place*, he thought, looking from one end to the other of the three-storied mansion.

The sweet smell of Honeysuckle filled the air. Michael inhaled deeply and looked out across the many gardens of bright red and white flowers located throughout the grounds. "Ahh," he said quietly to himself, "some day."

A large black and yellow bumblebee buzzed against Michael's ear, then his nose. He took off his hat and swatted wildly at the uninvited guest. "Get the hell outta here!" he said, ducking left, then right. The bee followed. "Damn it! Get outta here!" He looked up at the door and was surprised to find it open with a tiny gray-haired Asian woman standing in the doorway.

"Come in quickly!" she said. "Leave bee outside, please!"

Michael darted past her into a large entryway. "Thanks," he said turning to help her shut the door.

"No trouble," she said. "You OK?"

"I'm fine, thank you," he answered putting his hat on. Then, on a second thought he took it off again. The cool air conditioning felt good against his hot, wet skin. "I'm Detective Finder with the Indianapolis Police Department. Is Mr. Tanaka home? I would like to talk to him for a few minutes, if I could."

"Please," she said pointing to a row of shoes that lined the entry wall.

"Please?" Michael asked, completely baffled. "Ma'am?"

"Shoes please," she said, pointing towards her visitor's feet, then again at the wall.

"Oh ... Yeah ... I didn't think you still did that."

"Please."

"Well ..." Michael said, reaching down to untie his shoes. "When in Rome ..." He stood and kicked off his black dress shoes. His right big toe protruded through a ragged hole in his worn sock. "That's a bachelor for you," he joked, somewhat embarrassed.

"It's OK," the little lady said. "Toe now have better view of floor. Come."

The old woman turned and walked down three steps into what appeared to be a sitting room of some sort, simply decorated with a white sofa and white vases filled with eucalyptus cuttings. Michael tagged along behind her.

She crossed the sitting room and went through an open rice-paper door into a much larger, mostly unfurnished room. To the right, bright sunlight shone through an entire wall of windows overlooking a massive garden of multicolored flowers and shrubs outside. Each window was topped with thin paper shades that were rolled all the way up.

On the left was a long, bare wall. Near the middle, a heavy wooden pedestal stood against the wall. Atop the pedestal sat an elegant, handcrafted samurai sword in a black and gold sheath. The slightly curved sword, complete with gold handle, rested in a holder almost identical to the one Michael had seen in the museum.

Over half of the hardwood floor was covered by a large straw mat. Standing on the mat was, Michael assumed, Tanaka, along with a teenage boy. Both were dressed in white karate uniforms.

Tanaka appeared to be in his fifties. His salt-and-pepper hair was close cut and quite thin on top, but Michael still guessed him to be in prime shape for his age, or any age, for that matter.

The elder instructor and his younger student each held four-foot-long bamboo swords. The tense teenager awkwardly held his practice sword much like a baseball bat. He cautiously sized up his seasoned opponent, while moving in a wide circle from left to right.

"Excuse please," the lady whispered to Michael. "I have much to do now, so as to play bingo tomorrow on day off."

"Oh sure, go right ahead," Michael whispered back. "Don't let me stop you. I'll just stand here, if that's OK."

She bowed a short little bow and started to leave. Stopping, as if she remembered something important to tell the detective, the tiny woman turned back around toward Michael. "Psst ..." she signaled, lifting her full length silk gown and sticking out her left foot.

Michael curiously looked down at the gray wool footie she wiggled at him. There, at the end, was the top of her bare big toe, poking out through a little ragged spot. Michael grinned at the spry lady and bowed to her. She bowed, giggled, and slipped away.

Michael turned toward the teacher and student just in time to see the youth savagely strike down at his instructor with his bamboo sword held firmly in both hands. There was a loud clack as Tanaka calmly met and stopped the threatening sword with his own. The boy immediately recovered, withdrew, then quickly thrust his weapon straight toward the older man's chest. Tanaka's face was emotionless. He snapped himself sideways to the attack, allowing the student's sword to pass harmlessly in front of him.

In a blur, Tanaka spun, bringing his weapon sharply across the youngster's still-extended wrist. Twack! went the sound of bamboo against flesh and bone.

The boy cried out in pain as his sword bounced end over end across the straw mat. The instructor twirled his sword like a circus performer and brought it up horizontally at the neck of his stunned opponent. In the blink of an eye, Tanaka stopped his attack with the length of his practice sword just below the student's chin.

"Once again, you have caused yourself dishonor with your careless attack," he said to the boy. "You have allowed yourself to be separated from your sword."

Engulfed in shame, the student could only look at the floor.

Tanaka placed an assuring hand on the teenager's shoulder. "You are only guilty of learning," he said. "Do not be ashamed of failure. Benefit from your failures and try again. Pick it up ... Let us continue."

The boy retrieved his practice sword and again assumed a fighting stance.

"Remember," his instructor cautioned, "the sword is a part of you."

The boy nodded and began encircling his opponent. Tanaka was still very calm, holding his bamboo sword to his side. Suddenly, the young student brought his sword back in his right hand. He threw it, point first like a spear, at his teacher.

Tanaka made one sweeping move that sent the airborne weapon across the room.

"Now I am concerned," he said. "I must try to explain to your father that his son has a damaged brain. Did I not just say, 'Your sword is part of you?' If you were a boxer, would you tear off your arm and throw it at your opponent?"

"No sir."

"In the way of Fushigi Sh'Kata, a man would rather lose his entire hand still clutching the sword, than to have his sword fall alone to the floor by the blade of another. Yet now ... now you do the greatest disgrace of all. You willingly give away this precious part of your existence by throwing ... no, flinging it at your adversary. Does the painter throw his brush at the paper?"

"No sir."

"Think about what I am saying. Practice. Some day your father will proudly pass his sword down to you. But first you must learn the way of Fushigi Sh'Kata."

"Yes sir." The boy's head hung low in disappointment and frustration.

"You are a good student," Tanaka said, smiling for the first time. "You will learn, in time. Enough for today."

Teacher and student bowed to each other. The teen gathered his belongings and left through the garden door.

Michael extended his right hand, as the man he came to see approached. "Mr. Tanaka?" he asked.

"Yes, I am Sumio Tanaka," the soft-spoken man said, shaking his hand vigorously and bowing. "And whom might I have the honor of meeting?"

"I'm Michael Finder, with the Indianapolis Police Department. I'm a detective."

"Impressive."

Sumio Tanaka's English was flawless. If you were talking to him on the phone, you would never guess he was Japanese, Michael thought. The host walked to the sliding paper door, stepped aside, and gestured for Michael to enter the comforts of the sitting room.

"Thank you," Michael said. He hesitated when he started into the sitting room and turned slightly toward the empty matted area of the practice room. "Uhhmm ... I was wondering, Mr. Tanaka ... what was that you were teaching over there?" Michael pointed over his shoulder with his thumb.

"That is called Fushigi Sh'Kata."

"Fushigi Sh'Kata," the inquisitive detective repeated. "Very interesting ... or should I say, impressive."

"Whichever you chose," Tanaka said patiently. "Please." He again gestured through the paper doorway. "Have a seat. We can talk in here."

Pretending not to hear the second courteous offer to retreat to the sitting room, Michael casually strolled over to the edge of the straw mat. With his hands in his pockets, he appeared to slowly study the window shades, the mat, and the bamboo swords lying on the floor just off of the mat.

"May I?" he asked reaching for one of the wooden swords.

Tanaka nodded.

Michael wrapped his palms around the smooth bamboo handle. He shook the sword up and down as if trying to judge its weight.

"It's a bit heavier than I expected." Michael swung the rounded shaft at invisible targets. He studied the length of the sword balanced in front of him at eye level. Slashing here and there with playful enthusiasm, his eyes then focused past the bamboo, across the room, and on the polished black and gold sheath that encased the cold steal blade of the real samurai sword sitting in its stand.

"Now that's beautiful," Michael said, aborting his mock battle. Tucking the training sword under his left arm, he crossed the room and placed his face just inches from the priceless weapon of the ancient samurai. "May I look at this?" he asked turning to his host.

"Not to be rude, Mr. Finder ..." Sumio Tanaka spoke without moving from his place by the sliding paper door, "As a matter of custom and tradition, I prefer you not disturb that particular art piece."

"Oh sure ... I understand ... no biggie."

"Please, the handling of the Katana is one of a personal nature."

"I can respect that," Michael agreed. "I apologize. You have been very patient with my curiosity."

"Mr. Finder, I'm sure you are a very busy man. I cannot imagine you taking time out of your schedule to visit and admire my home furnishings. What brings you here?"

"Actually, Mr. Tanaka, I came to talk to you about two murders that occurred late last evening at the art museum."

"And what about these two murders?"

"Well, it appears that two men were killed during a burglary where some things from the Japanese art show were taken."

"What two men, Mr. Finder?"

"The museum director, Mr. Tiller, and a security guard named Bobby Kendall."

"I don't know these men."

"I didn't think you would, Mr. Tanaka."

"You said some things were taken. What things?"

"We don't know yet," Michael lied. "Why?"

"I have a great interest in many of the art objects from the museum showing."

"I've heard."

"Where have you heard?"

"A woman that works for the art store you used to partially own, Bonita Baker."

Tanaka quietly walked over to one of the big windows and stared blankly out across the gardens for a moment. "I don't know a Bonita Baker," he said. "How does she know me?"

"She said she had never met you. What she does know of you, she got mostly from records and other employees."

Tanaka nodded. "Then you know of Masato and me," he said.

"Ummm ... some. Why don't you tell me about it."

"There's not much to tell. The scenario fits many a childhood friendship, Mr. Finder. We grew up together, started a modest business together, began to experience some success, developed differences in opinions, and went our own ways in life."

"What sort of differences?"

"Business, Mr. Finder, just business. Masato's interest wandered from our art investment. He began to dedicate most of his time to his schooling in electronics and marketing."

"What's wrong with that?"

"Nothing. In fact, I was very proud of Masato. His grades were excellent."

"So, where did the disagreements come from?"

Tanaka slowly turned and faced Michael. "We divided our growing profits from our store in half," he said. "Almost all of Masato's money went towards school and later to start an electronics company that has now become the famous Ku-Tech that is flourishing today. I purchased a small home and re-invested my earnings back into the art store."

"I take it you were doing all the work, and not getting to enjoy any of the fruits of your labor," Michael said.

"Not quite so," Tanaka thoughtfully added. "I was happy. I had developed customers from all over the world. With a handful of part-time employees I was doing hundreds of thousands of dollars worth of trades a year. Masato was doing very well himself. He was quickly becoming a millionaire several times over."

"How did you feel about all that?" Michael asked.

"Even though his business was a great success, Mr. Finder, I was not unsuccessful. Somehow Masato began to change. He began to come into the art store once ... maybe twice a month and make major changes without telling me. When I would approach him about the changes..." Tanaka took a deep breath and exhaled. "We quarreled. He was selling priceless artifacts at a loss and hiring unneeded employees as favors to his business associates. These favors were stepping stones that were slowly elevating his company to where it is now."

"At your expense," Michael added.

"Yes. Exactly. At my expense," Sumio agreed. He turned and faced out the window again. "Masato no longer needed the money from his share of the art sales. When I offered to buy his half of the business, he refused. The only thing we both agreed on was that if our store were divided, it would only result in two smaller, unsuccessful art shops. I finally sold my half to him. With that, and what I saved on my own, I moved here."

"Why here, in Indianapolis?"

"My path led here. Plus, property is inexpensive. I am very

comfortable here."

"Where was it in Japan that you and Mr. Kudo grew up together?"

"Hiroshima."

"Hiroshima," Michael repeated softly. He looked up at the ceiling and tilted his hat back, trying to make some quick calculations of dates and years gone by.

"Yes, I was there when the bomb fell," Sumio said, "if that's what you are trying to figure. I was seven years old. Masato was eight. I can remember as clearly as if it were this morning."

"That must have really been terrible," Michael said.

"Terrible, Mr. Finder?"

Michael could see the reflection of Tanaka's face in the window. His features were twisting into what resembled a smile, but was in no way the product of anything pleasant or joking.

"Terrible?" he said again. "In one brilliant flash of light, Mr. Finder ... the brightest light you can ever imagine ... I lost my father, three older brothers, my mother, and a younger sister."

"I'm so sorry," Michael said. He was sincerely sorry.

"How could you have stopped such a thing? Anymore than I could have prevented the bombing of Pearl Harbor?"

"All those lives."

"Numbers are not important, Detective. Today you search for the killer of two people. On that day, in 1945, one hundred thousand people died in my city. Does that make your search any less important?"

"Not as far as I'm concerned. Two wrongs don't make a right," Michael answered.

"Exactly.   Each living thing is of equal importance. Unfortunately, in the eyes of war, living things are of equal unimportance."

"How did you survive ... I mean ... the blast. How did you live through it?"

"In the recklessness of youth, Masato and I had decided to abandon our lessons. We were up early that morning and had hidden on a train car to ride out near Tsuzu, to a dock on the Inland Sea. There we could frolic and talk to the fishermen. Trains ran all day, so we were never in fear of not being able to return. We were almost to where we were going to jump from the freight car when the whole world lit up. Not quite twenty miles from the city, and yet the light and heat were beyond comprehension." Tanaka lowered his head and became silent.

"I didn't mean to cause you to reflect back on such an unpleasant event." Michael could see the pain on his host's face. "I ... I was just curious. I've never known anyone who was actually at Hiroshima."

Sumio seemed to summon all the positive cheer that he could. He faced Michael and patted him lightly on the shoulder. "No harm done," he said. "Fate has turned life around, Mr. Finder. In my youth, Masato was like my brother. I loved him as a brother. America was the evil place that was responsible for killing our families. I hated Americans."

"And now?"

"Now? ... Now my brother shuns me, and treats me as if I were the very core of all unhappiness. I too have grown away from him. As I grew older and wiser, I learned how self-

destructive hatred can be. America is now my chosen home. I'm
even a U.S. citizen of several years. Ironic how events turn
around, wouldn't you say, Mr. Finder?"

"Things certainly have a way of turning on you," Michael
said. He reached under his suit jacket and drew his shining .357
magnum, pointed it safely across the room and carefully unloaded
the six heavy lead bullets. "This might be a bit out of line," the
detective said to the curious Tanaka, "but would you mind giving
me a little demonstration?"

"What sort of demonstration?"

"Well ... I was wondering," Michael put his empty handgun
back into his holster on his waist and handed the bamboo sword to
Tanaka, handle first, " ... Just how could you ... with a sword ...
defend yourself from a man with a gun?"

Sumio Tanaka gave no outward appearance of preparation
for the inquisitive detective's attack.

"Are you ready?" Michael asked, standing somewhat like
a gunslinger in an old western movie.

"A man practiced in Fushigi Sh'Kata is seldom unready,"
Tanaka said proudly.

Michael quickly gripped the butt of his gun with his right
hand and snatched it from his holster.

The only part of Tanaka's body that seemed to move was
the arm and hand holding the training sword. Completing a
blurring sweep, the bamboo fell hard against Michael's right wrist.
"Twack!" The room filled with the same sickening sound that had
been heard earlier when the youthful student had been disarmed.

"Oowwwhhh!!" Michael hollered. "Jeez ... us! That hurts

like hell!" His gun landed with a thump at the furthest corner of the straw mat. "Holy moly!" Michael grabbed his wrist. Waves of pain rippled through his arm. "Damn that hurts!"

"Are you all right?" Sumio calmly asked.

"Oh man." The embarrassed policeman held his wrist in his left hand and pushed them both down between his knees. "I think it's broken."

"It is not broken."

"Yeah it is."

"Mr. Finder, it is not broken."

"It is too."

"You really should be careful," Sumio said, examining Michael's wrist. "You could end up losing your hand someday ... or worse, your head."

"Yeah, you're right. Somebody already found that out," Michael mumbled as he went to get his gun.

The frustrated detective never realized until now how many things moved in a wrist when you tie your shoes, but he painfully managed to complete the task. He had finished his interview and was standing in the foyer. The spry, gray-haired woman that had saved Michael from the bee attack now balanced a small white plastic bag, filled with ice and water, on his throbbing hand and wrist.

"Feel better?" she asked.

"Yes, thanks again." Michael bowed slightly, adjusted the ice pack, and stepped out into the afternoon heat. He was opening the car door when he heard the familiar voice of Tanaka call out.

"Detective Finder, please wait!"

Michael stopped and looked out across the top of his tan Chevy. "What is it, Mr. Tanaka?"

"Excuse me ... but ...what did you mean when you said someone already knew about losing a hand or their head?"

The homicide detective thought for a moment. "I guess it won't matter if you know," he said halfway to himself. "One of the victims in this case I'm on was missing a head and a hand with a gun still in it."

"You have cleverly put me to a test."

"Sort of."

"I am a suspect now, no doubt?"

"Sort of."

"What should I do now, Detective Finder?"

"Whatever you want, I guess," Michael said. He got into his police car, started it up and adjusted the air-conditioning to the high position. The power passenger window on Michael's car hummed and slid down. "Mr. Tanaka!" he shouted.

"Yes, Detective?"

"Don't leave town."

Tanaka nodded his understanding, and Michael drove down the long driveway. Bonita should have plenty of flowers by now, he thought.

SEVEN

Hundreds of mourners were returning to their cars. Most walked silently. Some spoke quietly. And a few wept. Michael watched them all as Clevous Tiller's casket was slowly lowered into the grave. It was not inconceivable that the killer could be standing right there in Crown Hill Cemetery, watching or even participating in his victim's funeral.

Michael did not enjoy going to funerals of people he knew and liked, let alone strangers. The only reason he was at this one was for the chance of spotting a clue or two to help solve this case. He looked at Bonita standing solemnly at his side. She took him by the arm, gave a little pat and forced a smile on her troubled face. Well ... maybe not the only reason, Michael thought.

"You OK?" he asked her softly, placing his arm over her shoulder and gently pulling her closer.

"Yeah, I'm all right, but can we go now?"

"Sure, I'll take you back to the hotel. I've seen all I'm gonna see here this morning."

"Thanks, I'm not feeling so good."

"Do you want to stop and get a bite to eat ... it might make you feel better?"

"No ... I just want to go back to my room."

"Bonita!" a female voice called out from somewhere behind the couple.

A redheaded woman in her late thirties approached and took Michael's companion by her free hand. The woman's mascara was slightly streaked from a trickle of tears shed earlier.

"I thought that was you," she said. "How ya doin' Hon?"

"I'm all right, Connie," Bonita said reaching up and dabbing a tear from the redhead's cheek. "But what about you?"

"Ohh ... I'm OK. It's just that after working for that ol' goat for nine years I kinda got attached to him. It just hit me now, ya know?"

"Yeah, from the few times I saw him he seemed very nice."

"Oh, Clevous was all right I guess. He was great to work for. He let me get away with murd ..."

The redhead froze when she realized what she was saying. Her shoulders heaved, she held her handkerchief to her face to catch the flood of fresh tears that now poured down.

"I don't believe I said that," the woman sobbed.

"It's OK," Bonita said, trying to comfort her friend.

"I've got to stop thinking about it. My mascara must look like total hell," the woman said, wiping carefully beneath each eye. She lifted her head, took a deep breath and extended a right hand toward the handsome man that had been calmly standing by.

"I'm sorry," she said. "You must think I'm a big crybaby by now. I'm Connie."

"Oh no ... !" Bonita quickly interjected. "I'm sorry. I've been so rude ... Connie Prescot ... meet Michael Finder. Michael ... Connie."

"I wish we could be meeting under better circumstances," Michael said, shaking the offered hand. "I understand how you must feel."

"I'll be just fine," Connie said. "You must be the policeman friend Bo has been telling me about."

"I don't know ... am I?" Michael asked looking at Bonita.

The detective's green-eyed girlfriend gave a playful punch to his shoulder.

"You know you are," she said smiling.

Connie laughed for the first time. "Bonita was my party buddy for the last month or so," she said. "She got in town to set things up for the art show and we would go out almost every other night for drinks."

"You make me sound like a lush," Bonita said shyly.

"Ohh, it wasn't that bad," Connie continued. "But, if you could imagine, here's Clevous in Indianapolis pleased as punch that his museum was going to have a rare Japanese art show and Mr. Kudo is pleased that everyone is so receptive and so proud of his collection. Those guys were walking around with their chests stuck out, while Bo and I were working our butts off to make this thing work."

"We did it," Bonita smiled.

"We sure did, kid."

Connie paused for a moment. "I'm gonna miss you, Bo," she said. "You should be packed and ready to go about now, aren't you?"

"Well, we're all ready to leave, but ..." Bonita's sentence trailed off as she bit her lower lip and nervously looked at Michael.

The detective spoke up. "What she's trying to say is I've put a freeze on everyone's departure until I get a better idea of who killed your boss and the guard."

"Uh-huh," Connie said suspiciously. She stuffed her wet handkerchief into her purse. "That's a clever way to keep her in town. I've been after her all last week, but she seemed determined to leave ... that is, until your name started coming up, Michael."

"I assure you, the hold on the art exhibit is strictly business. But if Bo wants to stick around after this is cleared up, I wouldn't mind one bit."

Bonita blushed slightly. "Well, I must say Indianapolis has more reasons for me to stay than any other city we've visited on the tour. It's also been the most exciting."

"Do you have any idea who the murderer is?" Connie asked Michael.

"Well, I'm still working on a lot of things," he said.

"What's left to work on?" Bonita snapped. "I don't see why you just don't go and lock up this Tanaka guy and get it over with."

"You mean you have somebody?" Connie could hardly contain the excitement in her voice.

"I'll say he does."

"No, I don't. Not really."

"You do, Michael! You told me Tanaka nearly broke your wrist with that sword thing at his house the other day. He even admitted that he and Mr. Kudo didn't get along."

"I know, I know," said Michael. "I'm just not ready to commit myself until I have a little more evidence. Tanaka's not going anywhere and I need just a bit stronger case for court."

"Can't you go arrest him and then build your case?" Connie asked.

"No, it doesn't work that way."

"I don't know. I guess I'm just scared."

"Well don't worry, ladies. I'm doing the best I can. I want this guy as badly as anybody, but I'm going to do it right."

"I'm sorry," Bonita said. She reached over and gave Michael a peck on the cheek. "I guess I'm just a little scared and frustrated, too."

"What's Kudo think about all of this?" Connie asked Bo.

"Hell if I know. I haven't even met him."

"You still haven't met him after all you've done with the show and everything!"

"No, not even once."

"Well Hon, make your move." Connie nudged Bonita, then pointed out across the cemetery. "He's right over there ... been there all morning. Introduce yourself, make him notice you."

"What? Kudo's here!" Michael said, spinning. "Where? I need to talk to him."

"Right over there."

Connie pointed over rows of tombstones to a long silver limousine parked on a back drive of the cemetery.

"Connie, you're wonderful. I've been looking all over for this guy." He took Bonita by the hand.

"Want to meet your boss?" he asked.

"Sure, why not?"

"Nice meeting you," Michael said over his shoulder to Connie. "I may need a statement from you later."

"Fine," the redhead called out. "I'll probably be at the museum."

"Connie!" Bonita shouted back as she walked sideways trying to keep up with Michael. "I'll be in this afternoon to help you."

"I'll be there, Hon," Connie waved to the couple weaving between grave markers toward the limousine.

As Michael and Bonita approached the super luxury car, the driver's door swung open. A Japanese man in his early twenties stepped out. He was well dressed in an expensive but conservative gray business suit.

"How may I help you, sir?" he said, bowing.

"I'm Detective Finder with the city police department."

Michael pointed to Bonita beside him. "This is Miss Baker. She's an employee of Mr. Kudo's. We would both very much like to talk to him. Is he in there by any chance?"

"Yes, Mr. Kudo is here," the chauffeur said. "But I regret to inform you that he is very busy and will not be able to see you now."

"Sir, please ... you don't understand," Michael said attempting to hide his frustration. "We are investigating the murders of ..."

A rear door on the limousine opened unexpectedly. A slender, older man emerged from behind the dark tinted window of the car door. A full crop of professionally styled white hair handsomely adorned his Asian features. Black-rimmed glasses added a scholarly touch to his almost noble aura.

Michael recognized and appreciated quality in fashion. The man's five-foot nine-inch frame was tailor-fitted into a comfortable-looking black business suit. The fine weave of the material was foreign to the detective's trained eye.

The man closed the car door. The morning sun flashed sharply in a large diamond on his right middle finger. The diamond was the eye of a gold serpent curled around the band. The man said something in Japanese to the chauffeur, who delivered a crisp bow and silently stepped away.

"I am Masato Kudo," the man said in English to Michael. "I apologize for not being available for your interviews, Mr. Finder." His voice was soft and smooth.

"I'm just glad I finally caught up with you," Michael said. "I was beginning to think you weren't in town."

"I have been in and out of the city many times, Detective. I have a jet that allows me to be quite flexible with my travel needs."

"Here, sir," Michael said reaching into his suit jacket pocket and pulling out one of his cards. "I'd really like you to call me before you leave again, please."

"Of course." Kudo politely took the card. Turning to Bonita he said, "You must be the beautiful Miss Baker."

"I don't know about the beautiful part, but I am Bonita Baker," she said.

"I am honored to meet you, Miss Baker. Your work with the art tour has been magnificent."

"Thank you. I felt like you didn't want to see me."

"I assure you, Miss Baker, I would not have allowed you to leave my employment without a great feast to celebrate your many accomplishments. I could not have shared my art with this country without your help."

"Well, thank you. I'm pleased to meet you, sir."

Kudo bowed to Bonita. "Now, if you could please excuse us just a moment," he said. "I feel Mr. Finder has many questions for me that should be answered."

"Yes, sir, I understand," she said. "I'll be at the car, Michael."

"Shall I have my driver take you somewhere?" Kudo offered.

"No thanks. I can use the walk. It's not too far."

Michael pulled his keys from his pants pocket. "Take these, Bo," he said. "Start up the air-conditioning. I'll try not to be too long."

Bonita took the keys and started walking down the narrow curved drive. Michael and Masato Kudo watched the shapely blond until she was well out of hearing range.

"She is a very pretty lady," the older man said as Bonita disappeared around a grassy hill. "The two of you look well together."

Michael smiled. "Thank you, we've only met a few days ago though."

"Even so, I can tell you have some interest in the young woman."

"Yeah, I've enjoyed being with her the last couple of days. We seem to click somehow."

"Click?" Masato asked curiously looking at the detective. "Ahhh ... you get along. Correct?"

"Yeah, I guess that's what I mean. We get along."

"American slang is very complicated, but I am constantly amused by it."

"You speak English very well," Michael said.

"Thank you. I find being bilingual is more than helpful when doing business in America. I like to speak to my clients face-to-face. I believe they prefer it also."

"I would think so."

"Tell me, Mr. Finder, what progress are you making with the investigation?"

"Well, I'm checking into a strong lead, but I really need to talk to you about several things."

"I am at your service. I will answer all that I can."

The two men walked slowly among the tombstones. Michael, with his suit jacket open, had his hands in his pockets. Kudo held his hands loosely behind his back.

"Tell me about Sumio Tanaka, Mr. Kudo. Have you seen him since you've been here in Indy?"

"Yes, three times. Why, is Sumio involved in this case?"

"Possibly. It depends on what I can learn about him. I did talk to him at his home, but he neglected to tell me he had seen you."

"That is not surprising."

"Why? What happened, these three visits you're talking about?"

Kudo collected his thoughts briefly. "Each time I saw Sumio it was at the museum," he said. "He came in to see the collection. He once owned many of the pieces before he sold his share to me."

"I remember hearing that. Go on."

"When I first saw Sumio it was near the beginning of the show. I had not seen him for many years. He was looking at all of the displays. He told me it was like visiting Japan and that he often missed his birthplace. We spoke kindly together, Sumio and I. He even said that he may have been a bit hasty in his departure from our country."

"Why's that?" Michael asked.

"Sumio left in anger. He and I had much friction over business matters. He felt I was using too much of our profits on my personal goals. I offered him two million dollars, American money, for his half of our business. He quickly accepted and moved here to Indianapolis. A move I think he regrets."

"Why do you think that?"

"The actual value of the artifacts was much greater than the amount paid to Sumio. On his second visit, he offered to buy one of the art pieces back from me. When I refused, he became very upset and left."

"What piece was he trying to buy?"

"The Haiku Dragon. A beautiful jade sculpture."

"The same one taken from the museum?"

"The same."

"Get outta here!" Michael said to himself. He pushed his hat back on his head as he often did when he was thinking. After several seconds he broke the silence. "What about the third time? You mentioned a third visit."

"Yes, the last time he came into the museum was most unpleasant. When his final offer on Haiku was rejected, Sumio smashed a glass display case with his hands. Years of Fushigi

Sh'Kata have not tamed his raging temper. I was embarrassed for him. I told everyone that I accidentally dropped a packing crate on the display case."

"What about Fushigi Sh'Kata? What is that? We're not talking about some Ninja, karate cult, are we? We had some guy a few years back that thought he was a Ninja and hacked his roommate up with a sword."

"No, hardly that, Mr. Finder. Fushigi Sh'Kata is an art ... a way of life. Each move is precise. Each thought clear and accurate."

"Have you ever studied this art?"

"Yes, Sumio and I studied under Master Yasukya when we were perhaps eight or nine. As we got older I was forced to abandon Sh'Kata when my interest in school ... business ... and girls preoccupied my mind. Sumio, on the other hand, meditated and practiced constantly."

"This Master Yasukya, is he still around?"

"He has been dead many years past. Master was in his sixties when he first took Sumio and me under his wing. Both our families were killed in Hiroshima."

"I was told that. I'm sorry."

"Yes. Something that is not easily forgotten."

The two men reached the crest of a large grassy slope. Michael could now see to the other side of the lot. Almost a hundred yards away was his unmarked police car, engine running, with Bonita reclining in the passenger's seat.

"Mr. Kudo, you've known Sumio Tanaka for most of your life. Do you think he could kill, over the jade dragon?"

"If you are asking me if Sumio is capable," Kudo said, "I

would have to say yes. Sumio is quite capable of killing. However, if you wish to know my opinion on whether or not Sumio actually committed murder ... I don't know. He and I have been like brothers in the past, but we have been apart for a long time. Perhaps the years and bitterness have changed him. Do you think Sumio killed those men, Mr. Finder?"

"Well, it's beginning to look that way," Michael said reluctantly. "It's still just circumstantial evidence."

"What is circumstantial?"

"It's kind of like ... everything indicates Sumio Tanaka is most likely the best suspect, but I'm lacking hard physical evidence that says he is definitely involved in the murders. Do you understand?"

"I think so. Regardless, I have the utmost confidence in your crime-solving abilities. An article in your local paper indicated you were the best homicide detective the police department has to offer. Your chief spoke highly of you in the article."

"Thanks. I just try to do my best."

"It seems your best is very good. Is it true, you have never had a case unsolved?"

"Well, almost true. There was one case I lost, but that's another story."

"Still an excellent record."

"Thank you, Mr. Kudo. I have no intentions of messing up that record with this case." Michael anxiously looked out toward his car.

"I really need to get her back to her hotel room," he said. "Where are you staying, Mr. Kudo? I'll need to contact you for a written statement in a day or two."

"Of course. I am at the Omni, downtown. I have the penthouse suite."

"You mean the nine-room suite that takes up the entire top floor?"

"Yes, I find it most suitable for my needs."

"I guess," Michael said extending his right hand. "Thank you for your time."

"My pleasure," Kudo said, shaking the detective's hand and bowing. Michael returned an awkward bow and started for the car.

Similar to opening a refrigerator on a hot summer day, the coolness from the air conditioner poured over the detective's hot feet when he opened the car door. "That wasn't too bad, was it?" he said. Still standing outside, he removed his jacket, folded it neatly and laid it carefully on the back seat. He looked at Bonita. She was sitting in the passenger seat with her head back against the head rest. Her eyes were closed. She offered no response to the intrusion into the peace of the pleasantly cool cruiser.

Michael sat down in the driver's seat while he loosened his tie and unbuttoned the top button on his soggy dress shirt. "Ah, that feels better," he said slamming the door shut. "You ready to go?"

There was no answer.

"You OK, Bo?"

Michael reached over and placed his palm on her cold forearm.

No answer.

"Bo!" The tension began to rise in his voice. He shook her gently. "Bonita! Answer me!"

"Ummm ... you sure are noisy for a policeman," she finally said in a sleepy voice. "How in the world do you ever expect to sneak up on anyone?"

"Whew!" Michael whistled as he relaxed back into his seat. "Are you trying to give me a full head of gray hair?" he said.

"Oh, what's the matter?" Bonita said. "Did you think someone was going to get my head and hands or something?"

"Naw, you just scared me," Michael said. "There's something about this whole deal that gives me the willies. I feel like something really bad is coming up."

"I'm sorry. I shouldn't have said that. I haven't had anyone to worry about me for a long time. It ... well, it feels pretty good."

Bonita placed her hands on each side of Michael's face. She slowly brought her mouth against his. Michael was at first stunned by Bo's sweet aggression, but quickly adjusted. His hands slipped from the steering wheel. His fingers massaged her back, bonding their embrace. Her hair, her breath, the softness of her lips were all as Michael had imagined - delightful. They reluctantly ended their passionate kiss.

"I've been wanting to do that," Bonita confessed.

"What took you so long? I thought I'd never get a chance to do that before you got on a plane and flew back to Japan."

"I'm not gone yet."

Michael smiled and shifted the car into drive. He looked up the hill he had just come from. There at the top, barely visible, arms to his side, watching, stood Masato Kudo.

"What's he still standing there for?" Bonita said.

Michael slowly shook his head from side to side. "I don't know," he said softly then drove slowly toward the main gate of the cemetery.

EIGHT

Bursts of laughter echoed down the hallway from the homicide office. From the opposite end of the hall in front of the elevators, Michael could identify some of the unique laughs. There was Pete Zink's hicking chuckle, the baying-donkey style of Jimmie Wade, and four or five other basically normal laughs.

"Pay up!" somebody shouted.

"I don't believe it!" Dave West declared in his vibrant bass voice.

Pat Snider, the department's only female homicide detective, was saying something that couldn't quite be made out.

Michael walked through the doorway. His curiosity was in high gear. "What's going on?" he asked the group of detectives that were sitting in various positions and locations around a very disgusted looking Facts.

"Can you believe this guy?" Dave bellowed, pointing to Facts. The massive six-four black policeman took a sip from his "I'm A Monster" coffee mug.

"What?" Michael asked again. "What happened?"

Pete held his palms up and shrugged his shoulders. "Years ..." he said, "years I've known this guy, and he's never done this 'til now."

"Done what?"

Facts looked up at Michael and shook his head. "I couldn't remember an article from today's paper," he said.

"Facts lost a fifty-dollar bet with Jimmie," Pat added, as she poured herself another cup of coffee from a coffee pot that looked as if it hadn't been cleaned for a few months.

"Pay up!" Jimmie said smiling from ear to ear. He held his hand out to Facts.

Michael looked at his partner who peeled off two twenties and a ten and slapped them in the smiling detective's outstretched palm.

"You bet on your memory?" Michael said to Facts. "I thought you weren't going to do that."

"I know ... I know, I know!"

"Why isn't he supposed to do that?" Pete asked Michael.

"Ya want me to tell?" Michael asked his partner.

"I'll tell, it's no big deal," Facts said. He leaned to put his wallet away.

"Well, what is it?" Pete said, eagerly awaiting the answer.

"Pressure," Facts finally said. "Any kind of pressure and my noggin slams shut like a bank on Friday."

"You mean, just the pressure from a bet?" Dave's low voice came across the office.

"Well, yeah," Facts said, "but it's not the challenge, it's the chance that I could lose something."

"What in hell do you mean by that?" Pat said looking up from some folders on her desk.

"Yeah, well ... it's like ... Yo, Michael, help me outta this.

You know how it happens!"

All eyes turned toward Michael. He tipped his hat back slightly while carefully thinking of the right analogy.

"If you just tell Facts, 'I bet you can't remember this or that,' he probably can, because he has nothing to lose," Michael said. "On the other hand, if you bet money, or lunch, or put a gun to his head and said 'What's on page three? ...'"

"... I literally couldn't remember anything to save my life," Facts said finishing what Michael was trying to express.

"That is weird," Pat said, walking by Facts and pinching his cheek. "But we still love ya, Snookems!"

"Ain't that just like a woman," Facts said. "Ya do everything right, every day, and they won't give you two cents worth of their time. Ya start fuckin' up ... they love ya."

"Wait a minute!" Pat said. "That just means we have big hearts and that we can love a man in spite of his faults."

"Like hell," Facts said. "You take it as a sign of weakness. You realize it's safe to move in for the kill. I know how you girls think." He jokingly shook his head and finger at his female co-worker.

Pat snarled and hissed, clawing at the air in response to Facts' teasing.

"Watch out!" Facts shouted, throwing his arms over his head. "She's turning back into her natural form."

Pat laughed as Facts jumped from his chair and ran to a corner desk where Michael stood chuckling at their antics.

"Yo, Michael, did you see that?" Facts said. "Chased by another woman. They can't keep their hands off of me."

"Yeah, I don't know how you do it. You had better get a stick to carry around with ya."

"There you go. What an idea! I could ... I could, drill a hole in the end of it and tie a cord from the end of the stick to my belt. That way if I ever ..."

"Get outta here," Michael interrupted and bounced a wadded paper ball off of Facts' head.

"Hey careful! I don't have on my paper-proof vest."

"Speaking of paper," Michael said. "Have you seen the autopsy report yet?"

"I sure have. Do you want it verbatim or just the good stuff?"

"Just the good stuff for now."

"Check this out. The bullet that killed Tiller was fired by the security guard."

"What!?"

"I know. I scratched my noodle on that one also, but I double checked. The ballistics match. The guard's gun had been fired, and there was powder all over the hand. Whattaya make of that?"

"Why in the hell would the guard shoot Tiller?" Michael wondered out loud.

"Maybe the guard was in on the whole thing," Facts said. "There were no signs of forced entry. The guard could have let the bad guys in for a cut of the action. Guards don't make that much, ya know."

"A cut of the action is *exactly* what he got."

"Maybe he eighty-sixed Tiller when Tiller stumbled across them. Then the bad guys figured the guard was too hot for them to try an' cover up, so ... chop, chop."

"That's possible, but we checked the guard's record. It was clean as a whistle. You usually don't go from sparkling clean to murder and burglary."

"What if he thought Tiller was one of the burglars?"

"You mean, an accident?"

"Maybe." Michael slipped his hands in his pockets. With his hat tilted back, he stared blankly at the floor. "I don't know," he said. "Right now, Sumio Tanaka is our strongest suspect. Perhaps if we could find a connection between Tiller and Tanaka, we could piece more of this together."

"I checked on Tanaka. I checked on everyone, for that matter," Facts said. "It's not easy calling Japan. I had to call at one o'clock in the morning, our time, just to catch everyone at work, their time."

"What did you find out?" Michael asked.

"Nothing spectacular. Pretty much what he told you. I did find out that he gives a lot of his money to charities. A few boys' clubs here in Indy and a hospital in Hiroshima, on a regular basis."

"Heartwarming."

"Yeah, he's squeaky clean. No record at all and no formal education beyond our equivalent of high school."

"What about Masato Kudo?"

"Well," Facts started. "Aside from being damn near impossible to locate, Japanese people love him. He's *the* wealthiest man in Japan, and one of the wealthiest men in the world. He's brought a lot of money and jobs to his country."

"I talked to him today."

"You talked to Kudo? Where?"

"At the cemetery, he was at Tiller's funeral."

"What did he have to say?"

"A few things, but first tell me more about what you found out."

"Well, the usual rich guy stuff. Rags to riches story. His family was wiped out when we dropped the big one on Hiroshima. He paid for his education himself, started an electronics business, then, zoom ... he's got fingers into everything."

"Like what?"

"TVs, radios, computers. He's got two communication satellites up there somewhere for all kinds of cable networks. Ku-Tech Enterprises, his major corporation, owns or controls hundreds of smaller businesses all over the world. Ku-Tech even holds eight percent of all of the contracts with NASA for the next ten shuttle flights. It goes on and on. Do you need more?"

"You know, that's amazing," Michael said. "Everyone's heard of Ku-Tech Enterprises, but I had no idea it was that big."

"Big?" Facts said. "It doesn't come right out and say it, but Ku-Tech is probably the largest electronics set-up in existence."

"Does Sumio Tanaka fit into any of that big business anywhere?" Michael asked.

Facts shook his head. "Not one bit. The only connection

between Tanaka and Japan is when he worked at the art shop there. The rest of the time he's been right here in Indy, under our noses, living a low-key lifestyle, working in his gardens, and teaching that Fushigi Sh'Kata stuff."

"Did you, by any chance, ask about that when you were talking to the police in Hiroshima?"

"Sure did."

"And?"

"Never heard of it."

"Nothing at all?"

"Nope. I even asked a couple of our guys that have Japanese roots."

"Still nothing?"

"Right again."

"Get outta here. No one's heard of this?"

"Not anyone I can find."

"What about wives? Have Tanaka or Kudo been married?"

"Tanaka hasn't. Kudo's wife died of cancer several years ago."

"Any children?"

"Nope."

"Damn! I wish I could find just a little piece of good, solid evidence that would nail Tanaka, so I can get this solved and start enjoying my free time again."

"Did you ever enjoy free time?"

"Yeah, but not as much as I plan to after this is cleared up."

"Doing what?"

"Well ... you know, fun things."

"The only fun thing I can think of that you've been doing lately is a blond bombshell named Bonita."

Michael smiled and pulled his chair away from the desk. He sat down, rocked back, and laced his fingers together behind his head.

"Facts ol' buddy," he said, "I like her more and more as time goes by."

"I'm happy for ya," Facts said. "It's about time you started seeing someone again. I was beginning to think you were becoming a homo or something ever since you broke up with Sherry."

"Yeah, I know," Michael said. "I just don't seem to be able to hang on to a woman. It's like they're not from around here at all."

"Yo, Bonita's from Japan. What about that?"

"I meant this galaxy."

"Oh ... that narrows it down. You just want a nice little earth girl."

"Yeah, with teeth and hair and boobs, and believe it or not, a personality."

"Well, I got three outta four. I guess that's not too bad."

"What are you saying? Joan has a great personality."

"I was talking about her boobs. She's got no boobs. They used to be bigger. I think the kids sucked 'em off when they were born, the greedy little buggers. Now if I were ..." Facts paused and looked at the office door. "Do you know this guy?" he whispered and nodded toward a man who had just stepped into the chaotic homicide office.

Michael swiveled his chair in the direction Facts was indicating. "This is a twist," he whispered back to his partner.

"Who is it?"

Without answering, Michael stood and offered his right hand to the elderly Asian man dressed in brown pants, short sleeved shirt, and tie.

"Well, Mr. Tanaka," Michael said. "This is an unexpected surprise. What can we do for you?"

"Mr. Finder, I hope I'm not interrupting anything," Sumio said, shaking the detective's hand. "I've been thinking, and I feel we should talk."

"No problem," Michael said and placed his hand on Facts' shoulder. "Sumio Tanaka, this is my partner, Detective Brown. Do you mind if he listens in on this talk of ours?"

"Not at all," Sumio said, firmly shaking Facts' pudgy hand. "My pleasure, Mr. Brown."

Michael was secretly amused by Facts' apparent awkwardness with the little bow Sumio gave with his handshake.

"Likewise, Mr. Tanaka," Facts said.

Michael gestured toward a metal folding chair beside his desk.

"Here, have a seat," he said.

Tanaka sat and politely waited for the detectives to do the same.

"What's on your mind?" Michael asked.

After a brief pause Sumio began to speak, "I have been thinking," he said. "These murders you've told me about, I may know something about them."

"Is that right?" Michael said looking over at Facts.

"Yes, I believe I know who is responsible."

Michael sat up straight in his seat and held his hand to stop Tanaka. "Hold it!" he said. "Before you go any further, I think I'd better give you your Miranda warnings."

"Miranda?"

"Your rights, Mr. Tanaka," Facts explained.

"Am I under arrest?" Sumio asked, with a slightly worried tone to his voice.

"No, Mr. Tanaka," Michael said. "This is just a formality before we question you."

Confused, Tanaka looked from Facts to Michael.

"Mr. Tanaka," Michael continued, "you have the right to remain silent. You have the right ..."

"Please, Mr. Finder!" Sumio interrupted. "Don't insult me with your legal procedures. I came here only to help you, not to confess to a crime I didn't commit. I am a man of honor. Time is not on our side. Don't play games with me."

"Play games with you?" Michael shouted. "Don't you play games with me, Tanaka! I don't know if you realize this mister, but when we add up all the little details to this case, you don't come out looking too good, if you catch my drift!"

"It all depends on who's doing the adding," Sumio said.

"You are making a mistake."

Michael jumped to his feet. "How in the hell am I making a mistake?" he asked. "When it comes right down to it, I think you're a murderer!"

Sumio jumped to his feet. "That's the mistake I'm talking about!" he said.

Facts slowly got out of his chair and walked around the edge of the desk. "Whoa, guys." he said. "C'mon now, let's not get crazy here. Settle down."

"I apologize," Sumio said, seating himself in the folding chair again.

Michael remained standing. Hands in his pockets, he paced slowly behind his desk. "Did you visit with Masato Kudo several times during the art show?" he asked.

"Yes," Sumio answered.

"Did the two of you get into an argument?"

"Yes."

"Was it over the jade Haiku Dragon?"

"Yes."

"And did you break a display case in anger, during that argument?"

"Yes."

"Then why in the hell didn't you tell me that when I talked to you the first time?"

"Because you would think I killed those men!"

"I do think you killed those men!"

"See?"

Michael threw his arms up in the air, shook his head and looked at Facts. "Hell, I don't know," he said. "If you're innocent, Sumio, why the secrets? Sooner or later we would figure everything out."

"Sooner or later may be too late," Sumio said. "As I said before, time is not on our side. The longer you spend suspecting me, the more freedom you provide for the true assailant."

"OK," Michael said, sitting down and rolling his chair up to Sumio. "I'm game, who is the true assailant, as you call him?"

"First," Sumio started, "do you take pictures of the victims like I have seen on television?"

"Yeah, why?" Michael asked.

"May I see the pictures for this case?"

"We can't do that, Mr. Tanaka," Facts said. "Plus, I'm not so sure you would really want to see them anyway."

Tanaka calmly sat and stared at Michael. Facts walked over to a file cabinet and picked up a thick manila folder from the top. He held the folder in his hands and waited. Michael pushed with his feet and rolled backwards in his chair until it bounced off of the wall behind him. He folded his arms across his chest, puffed his cheeks full of air, and slowly let the air hiss through his pursed lips while he looked at the ceiling.

"All right," Michael finally said, "let him see some of the pictures."

"I knew you were going to say that," Facts said reaching into the folder.

"What do you need to see these for?" Michael asked.

"Just a moment," Sumio said, as Facts lay a stack of photos in front of him.

"I'm telling ya, these are pretty gruesome, Mr. Tanaka," Facts said.

"It doesn't matter," Sumio said as he quickly flipped through the pictures. His face was emotionless as he shook his head slowly.

"These limbs were removed with a single motion, were they not?" he asked without looking up.

Michael looked at Facts, knowing that he had read the full autopsy report. Facts silently nodded his head, confirming Sumio's statement.

"That's right," Michael said. "What else?"

"A very sharp blade. Razor sharp."

Again Facts nodded to Michael.

"Go on," Michael said.

Sumio shuffled through the stack of photos until he came to a picture of Clevous Tiller sprawled on the museum floor. "This man has not been mutilated," he said. "What was his cause of death?"

"You tell me," Michael said coldly.

"I would imagine shot. Probably by the other victim."

"How could you possibly know that?" Michael said. "You're building a nice little stack of evidence against yourself, Sumio. The only way you could know these things is if you were there."

"Not true, Detective."

"Then how?"

"It is the way."

"The way of what?"

"Mizu Kokoro."

"Who the hell is Mizu Kokoro?"

"A person who has reached the greatest height of Fushigi Sh'Kata becomes Mizu Kokoro."

"Wait a minute," Facts interrupted. "Let me make sure I'm still with it here. You're trying to tell us that you think the murderer is a person that turns into someone else. Kind of like ... uhh ... like a werewolf."

"Not at all, Detective," Sumio said. "Mizu Kokoro exists within an already skilled Fushigi Sh'Kata master, as an *addition* to his own personality. Not a replacement."

"Sort of like, 'samurai helper'," Facts said with a chuckle.

Sumio turned sharply to face Michael again.

"I assure you, Mr. Finder, this is not a joke!" he said.

Facts stood behind their irritated visitor and rolled his eyes in response to Sumio's theory.

"Look, Mr. Tanaka," Michael said trying to suppress a smile, "how could a person skilled in Fushigi Sh'Kata allow such a thing as Mizu to take over his mind?"

"That is the ultimate goal of the Sh'Kata warrior. To join with Mizu Kokoro."

"Is that what happened? Did you join with Kokoro and kill these men?"

"No, Mizu Kokoro has not yet seen me fit to share his company."

"Why would you want to share company with him?"

"Mizu Kokoro is no more evil or good than the person he possesses. Apparently the one you seek is of a great evil. Great enough for me to sense its strong presence."

"Well," Michael said. "That's a very interesting story, Mr. Tanaka. We'll keep an eye out for anybody with an extra person inside them."

"If you think I'm crazy, if you think I'm a murderer, why haven't you arrested me, Mr. Finder?" Sumio asked staring Michael in the eyes.

"I think that's a fair question," Facts said looking nervously from Tanaka to Michael.

The smile completely faded from Michael's face. "I don't know," he said after a full minute of silence. "I really don't know."

"Am I free to go?" Sumio asked.

Michael stood and again started pacing with his hands in his pockets. Facts was playing with his handcuffs in anticipation of Michael's answer.

"Why did you say we don't have much time, Sumio?" Michael asked as he stood with his back to the office, looking out of the window across the Indianapolis skyline.

"Once Mizu Kokoro is on the move, his task will soon be complete. No more than a few days."

"What is his task?" Michael stared out the window.

"There is no way to tell, but I can promise you, it will be bigger than a simple case of murder, Detective."

Michael never turned away from the window. "Go home, Mr. Tanaka," he said. "I'll call you when I need you."

"You'll need me sooner than you think, Mr. Finder."

"Oh yeah? Why's that?"

"You might be able to find him, but you won't be able to stop him."

"I'll take my chances."

Tanaka bowed slightly to Michael and Facts, then turned toward the office door.

"One of the differences between your werewolf and Mizu Kokoro, Mr. Brown ..." he said, looking back at Facts.

"What's that?"

"... Kokoro is real."

Sumio crossed the office and went out into the hall.

"You gonna let that nut go?" Facts asked Michael.

"Yeah, everything looks good here in this office, but a month or two from now, what kind of case would we have in court? When I can nail him good I'll make my move."

"Well, let me know," Facts said. "The sooner the better. We can get a break and go fishin' or something."

"Yeah," Michael said. He sounded distant.

"Ya know what?" Facts said, placing an arm over his partner's shoulder. "I've worked with you long enough to know when something's bothering you. Ya wanna tell me about it?"

"Something about this case worries me."

"Don't sweat it. You haven't lost one yet."

"Yeah, whatever. I'm gonna grab a sandwich downstairs.

Ya want one?"

"Sure, hang on ... damn. Hiroshima demonstrations," Facts said snapping his fingers.

"What are you talking about?"

"The article I couldn't remember this morning. It's about the demonstrations against the bombing of Hiroshima. They have 'em every year. The anniversary is coming up in a few days and a group of yo-yo's get together and spray paint their shadows on the sidewalks or buildings. Page five, second column over. Wouldn't you know I'd remember now?"

"Hiroshima," Michael muttered to himself. "I've heard that name more this week than I have in my whole life. Let's get outta here."

NINE

Sumio immediately sensed them waiting in the dark entry of his home as he shut and locked the front door. One of the four was closer than the others. Much closer. Sumio reached into the blackness and in one smooth sweep, flicked the plastic light switch with his index finger. The foyer lights came on instantly, confirming what was already known. A tall, skinny man in a black suit stood just a few feet away, with a blue steel revolver leveled at Sumio's head.

"Don't move, Chink!" he said. "Just take it real easy." His voice was high and feminine. His features were slender and unhealthy. His big ears and short brown hair made him resemble a rat or weasel.

"What do you want?" Sumio asked. "I do not keep money in my house."

The lamps in the sunken sitting room off of the foyer came on, illuminating three men standing around the glass coffee table. All three were large, but Sumio's attention was quickly drawn to the largest of the men. This one was every bit of seven feet tall. His build easily qualified him as a modern-day Neanderthal. Long hairy arms, protruding forehead and everything.

"We don't want your money, Chinaman. We just want you to join our little party," said the man to the left of the Neanderthal. He was in his late twenties and had black hair. His gloved hand was wrapped around the bottleneck of Sumio's finest saki, which had been stored in the liquor cabinet.

"Come on, get your ass down here!" he said, taking a drink from the bottle, then wiping the sleeve of his suit across his mouth.

The weasel gestured with his gun. Sumio moved down the steps into the sitting room with the other intruders.

The fourth man, along with the Neanderthal, had remained silent. He sat on the edge of the couch with his arms folded. He had blond wavy hair and a trimmed mustache. Beside him, on the floor, sat a large black leather suitcase and a smaller tan canvas bag. "Get on with it!" he said in a heavy German accent.

"What do you want?" Sumio again asked the saki drinker.

"Oh, it's not what we want. It's what the person that hired us wants."

"What is that?"

"Well now, we're not allowed to tell you too much for some reason. I personally don't see what difference it'll make. But, if it'll make ya feel any better though, we're getting paid a lot of money to see to it that you don't live through the night." He took another sip from the bottle.

"I guess you just pissed off the wrong person," the weasel said, slowly returning his gun to its shoulder holster. He reached into his suit pocket and brought out a heavy folded knife. With the press of a button, eight inches of stainless steel clicked into view. "One little wave of my magic wand and it will all be over, Chinaman," the weasel said.

"I am Japanese."

"Makes no difference to me, it pays the same."

"Finish this, and let's go," the German barked. "I don't like the smell of this at all. Something's not right. Four of us for one little oriental?"

"Relax, Sauerkraut," the saki drinker said. "Lenny, put our friend's worries to rest, would ya, so he can quit whining about the biggest 'piece-of-cake' job we ever had."

The weasel smiled as he brought the blade of his knife up to about face level. "Good-bye," he quietly hissed to his victim.

"Good-bye," Sumio calmly said, with a slight bow.

The weasel lunged forward, thrusting the blade of his knife towards Sumio's throat.

"Snap!" went the sound of Lenny, the weasel's, wrist as Sumio caught and broke it in the blink of an eye.

"Yaaahhh!" the henchman screamed, grabbing his crippled limb. The knife was still held loosely in his twitching fingers.

"I knew this was too easy!" the German shouted, raising a nine millimeter automatic from under his suit coat.

Sumio positioned himself between the screaming weasel and the German, then froze. The German pointed his gun at the easy target, and pulled the trigger, but Sumio was no longer where he had been. The shot missed Sumio and entered the gaping mouth of the weasel, sending skull fragments, brains, and blood spraying across the white wall in the background.

"You stupid ass!" the saki drinker screamed at the German. "You shot Lenny!"

As the weasel's body flopped to the floor, Sumio plucked

the knife from the falling dead man's fingers.

"To hell with Lenny. Help me shoot this fool!" the German ordered, as he fired at Sumio and again missed.

The saki drinker threw down the bottle and drew a snub-nose .38 from his belt. "Shit!" he said, then fired two shots at Sumio. Both missed. "Shit!" he said again. "This is getting out of hand!"

Sumio's arm blurred forward, launching the borrowed knife in the direction of the blond gunman. There was a "thump" as the blade buried itself into the German's chest, piercing and stopping his heart. After firing one last shot into the floor, the German stumbled back two steps, then fell, crashing through the glass top of the coffee table.

The saki drinker and the Neanderthal raised their arms to shield themselves from the thousands of shards of glass that burst outward. Sumio, taking advantage of the distraction, sprang from the sofa to the opposite side of the room, then dove head first through the paper door that divided the sitting room from the matted workout area.

"Shit!" the saki drinker said and stomped his foot in frustration. He ran to the torn opening in the paper door and peered into the unlit practice room where Sumio had disappeared. "You're all mine, ya little Jap!" he shouted into the opening. "Ya hear me?"

There was no answer.

The gunman looked at the bodies of his dead colleagues, then at the Neanderthal. "Tea Box," he said. "Looks like this little guy just doubled our share of the money. What-da-ya-say we go in here and collect?"

The Neanderthal smiled and slowly nodded his understanding. He held in his massive hand what had to be the world's largest handgun. In two strides he was beside his partner. With just his left hand he grasped the frame of the sliding door, ripped it from its track and flung it across the room.

The two men stepped through the doorway and paused briefly while their eyes adjusted to the darkness. Aided slightly by the light from the sitting room, they could barely make out Sumio standing in the center of the practice mat. His left hand held the priceless samurai sword, still in the beautiful curved black sheath that protected the blade.

"Well ... what 'cha got there, Jap?" the saki drinker said, inching closer to the motionless Sumio. He waved the other giant gunman around toward the Asian's back. "Look here Tea Box, our Jap's gone an' got himself somethin' to fight with."

The Neanderthal eased in behind Sumio, about ten feet away, pointing his hand-held cannon from the waist.

"That's not gonna do you much good against this," the saki drinker said, bringing his .38 up to the Fushigi Sh'Kata instructor's chest. He sent the message to his finger to pull the trigger about the same time Sumio moved.

With a shuffle more than an actual step, Sumio shortened the distance between himself and the smaller gunman. The cold blade silently escaped from the sheath, flicked an invisible circle through the darkness, then returned to the sheath as quietly as it had left. Something heavy bounced on the straw mat below, and what sounded like a water faucet came on.

"Shit!" the saki drinker yelled when he was unable to fire his gun for the second time. He turned slightly toward the light coming from the sitting room to see what the problem was. "Aww shit!" he screamed. His entire hand was gone. Where it had been was now a splattering fountain of warm blood, pouring across the floor.

"My ... my ... my hand!!!"   The panicking gunman desperately and unsuccessfully tried to stop the flow of the precious fluid from his shaking stump with his other hand. "Tea ... Tea ... Tea Box!" blurted the saki drinker. "Tea Box. My ... my fucking hand!"

The Neanderthal growled with rage as he pointed his cannon pistol at Sumio's back and pulled the trigger. A flame two feet long, combined with a deafening blast, ripped through the tranquil dojo. Sumio dodged to the left. The blazing ball of lead meant for him slammed into the chest of saki drinker like the kick from a wild horse. The force of the large bullet's impact plowed completely through the attacker's torso, knocking him out of his shoes and into a paneled wall. A faint gurgle was the only sound before he died.

Sumio spun, and again his blade lashed out into the darkness. A large black gun, along with an even larger hand sailed across the matted area.

Tea Box held up his handless arm and roared. Clenching his remaining fist, he charged the smaller man. Keeping the sword in the sheath, Sumio drove the handle upwards into the chin of the ape-like gangster. Unaffected, Tea Box squeezed his powerful fist around the sheath of the ancient sword and attempted to wrestle it from its master.

Sumio gripped the handle of the sword with both hands and snatched the weapon from its captured casing. The light from the adjoining room flashed briefly along the metal blade as Sumio flicked the sword to the right, then left, coming against and through the Neanderthal's neck. A thick scarlet jet sprayed the ceiling as Tea Box's head tumbled sideways to the matted floor.

Sumio retrieved the sheath, returned the sword, and calmly walked into the sitting room and picked up the phone. He pushed the three digit emergency number and listened for the ringing on the other end.

"Hello," he said when the dispatcher answered, "I believe I will need the police. ... Yes ... I'll wait." Sumio shook his head in disbelief that he was actually put on hold.

He placed his hand over the mouthpiece and looked in the foyer. The front door was now standing open, slowly creaking as the hot night air brushed it back and forth. Sumio stared into the night. He couldn't see anything out there. He couldn't hear anything except the wind agitating the leaves and flowers in the gardens. A moth had flown in, and was now spastically fluttering around the dim foyer light.

"I know you're there," he whispered under his breath in Japanese.

TEN

"OK Sumio, let's start one more time."

"Why again, Michael? What haven't I said that you want to hear?"

"I just need to hear your story again. There seem to be some unanswered questions," Michael said, taking a sip of his diet cola. "The average citizen doesn't come home from a day on the town to find four hit men waiting in the living room."

"I can understand, but I still don't know any more about why they were there than you."

"Yo, Michael!" Facts came bolting through the homicide office door. "Oh ... sorry, are you taping this?" he asked, pointing back and forth between Michael and Sumio.

"Naw, we haven't even gotten that far yet," Michael said. "What have you found out?"

"You were right about the big guy with no head. He's Thackery 'Tea Box' Mooney. Usually does mob-related hits out of Chicago. Arrested seven times for murder. Never convicted. He was a suspect only once here, and that was on the Jack Tubbs murder case in '81."

"What about the guy that was in the room with Tea Box?"

"Mike Pacos. A real loser. He tried a little bit of everything. Never made big time. He was from around Chicago also."

"The others from Chicago too?"

"No, the one with the back of his head all over the wall was a local named Lenny Beanblossom. I've never heard of 'im, but some of the uniform guys said he hung around the Southside. He did a few years for slicing up a man during a robbery. Then he got extra time for cutting a prisoner's throat. Real sweet guy. The fourth one nobody knows. Our only lead is from the F.B.I. They think he could be a pro from Germany that landed in New York a few days ago. Then they lost him. We're sending pictures now."

"Thanks," Michael said. He tossed his pen down on the desk and rocked back in his swivel chair. "Well Sumio, you've heard the line up. Did you know any of those guys?" he asked.

"No, not at all."

"Have you ever been around Chicago?"

"Never."

"Not even once?"

"No, never."

"Looks like we're gonna be here a while. Can I get you something to drink?" Michael asked.

Sumio took a deep breath and let it out. "Water would be nice, I suppose."

"I'll get some," Facts said. He started for the door.

"Watch out. Comin' through!" A hefty voice warned from the hallway.

Facts jumped to the side. "Yo! What 'cha got there, Randy?" A crime lab technician dressed in a navy blue police jumpsuit rushed in carrying a large black leather suitcase and a smaller brown canvas bag.

"Over here," Michael said, clearing the top of his cluttered desk.

"Wait 'till you see this," the technician said. "I was on my way to the property room with this stuff, but I knew you would want to see it now."

"From the house?"

"Yeah, we took tons of pictures before we moved anything. Do ya mind me bringing these here?"

"No not at all," Michael said. "I'm glad you did." He looked at Sumio sitting calmly in the folding chair beside the desk. "Have you seen these before?" he asked.

"These bags were with the men who were in my house tonight."

"What's in them?"

Sumio smiled, "I don't know."

"What's funny?"

"Nothing's funny. I am just amused by your attempts to catch me in a lie," Sumio said. "Your approach is so ..."

"Is so what?" Michael asked, in a quiet but firm voice.

"So ... wrong!" Sumio answered with sternness.

Michael sat back and tipped his hat up as he had done so many times before. "Well ... let's have a look," he said, unzipping the black case and folding the top back. "Good gigglely-wigglely!"

Michael said and whistled.

"Ain't that somethin'?" Randy said, running his hand across the thick stacks of hundred dollar bills.

"Jeez!" Facts hollered, leaning over Sumio's shoulder to get a better look at the suitcase stuffed with money. "How much is that? Oh ... sorry, Mr. Tanaka." Facts realized he was leaning on the annoyed Japanese man's shoulder.

"What is this?" Michael asked as he thumbed through the crisp packets of cash. "About a hundred grand?"

"At least," the technician added.

"How 'bout it, Sumio?" Michael flipped the ends of the bills from one of the bundles. "Is it a hundred grand? More maybe?"

"I don't know."

"What have we here?" Michael knocked a few of the bundles out of the case and pulled a piece of white paper from between the other stacks of money.

It was a note. Neatly in the center of the paper was the message: "For Mr. Sumio Tanaka. A job well done."

Michael handed the note to Facts who read it along with Randy.

"A job well done," Michael said, lacing his fingers together in front of his nose and peering over them at Sumio. "What did you do that someone would pay you this much money?"

Sumio silently read the note Facts held in front of him. "I don't understand. I honestly don't understand," he said, looking from one detective to the other.

The office was quiet as Michael probed through the rest of the suitcase. He put all of the bundles back in place. Took another sip of his cola, frowned, and tossed the rest of the can into the metal trash basket beside him.

"What else do we have here?" Michael said. He reached and picked up the brown canvas bag. It was heavy and whatever was inside was hard. Michael loosened the draw string around the top, gripped the rough object and pulled the canvas away. It was a sculpture. A finely detailed dragon carved from jade. The fierce gaping jaws were precise to each tooth. Every scale on the curled serpentine body was visible. A true masterpiece of ancient art.

"Gentlemen," Michael said. "I believe what we have here is the Haiku Dragon."

"From the museum," Facts added.

"Yeah, and something else ..." Michael set the green dragon carefully on his desk and picked up the flat square plastic case that had fallen out. "This was in the bag with the dragon," he said, turning the case from side to side.

"What's that?" Facts asked.

"I don't know. 'United States Army ... Top Secret'." Michael read from the side of the case. "It looks like a disk from a computer or something. What the hell *is* this?" He held it out to Sumio.

"I don't know, Michael."

"Oh come on, Sumio!" Michael shouted. "Cut the bullshit. You know what the hell this is!"

"How could I?"

"How? I'll tell you how. Those dead guys didn't bring *all* of this stuff with them. I bet they brought the money, but you already had the Haiku Dragon."

"That's not true. They had the bags with them. No one even mentioned the suitcase or the other bag. I just noticed them next to the sofa with the man Detective Brown said was most likely a German."

"Yeah, right. Well, I see things different. I know you went to Masato Kudo and tried to get Haiku from him. I imagine you found a buyer and realized an opportunity to make a quick hundred thou'."

"Not true."

"I don't know about this 'Top Secret' thing, but I figure you went to the museum to get the dragon yourself."

"No Michael, I didn't."

"You didn't count on the security guard and Tiller stumbling across you. You were trapped."

"No."

"You broke the display case with the sword in it and used it to kill them."

"No!"

"You killed them in the same unique, efficient manner that you killed those men tonight!"

"No! No! No!" Sumio jumped to his feet.

Michael knocked his chair back and stood to face Sumio's aggression.

"If I'm guilty of that ridiculous scenario, then why would

I kill these men tonight in my own home and call the police myself?" Sumio asked.

"They were probably bringing the money to close the deal and something went wrong. I'm not sure what, but something 'happened'." Michael pulled his handcuffs from his belt. "You're under arrest," he said. "Turn around and put your hands behind your back. You're charged with murder and burglary."

Sumio just stood and stared into Michael's eyes. Facts and Randy came from behind the Fushigi Sh'Kata instructor and each took hold of his arms. Reluctantly, Sumio turned and Michael quickly cuffed his wrists together.

"You are making a serious mistake," Sumio said over his shoulder.

"Yeah, well, I've been told that before," Michael said. "Randy, would you mind escorting Mr. Tanaka down to Turn-Key. I'll be down later with the rest of the paperwork and the stuff from the house."

"Sure, Michael." The technician gave Sumio a gentle push and led him towards the door.

"There *is* something I haven't told you," Sumio said softly as he was led away.

"Hold on a second!" Michael said. "What haven't you told me?"

Sumio turned to face the detective. "There was a fifth person at my home this evening," he said.

"Who?"

"It is someone I have tried to warn you about."

Michael looked blank for a moment, then his eyes lit up. "Oh yeah! Our little invisible friend, what's his name?"

"Mizu Kokoro," Facts said.

"Yes, of course! Mizu Kokoro! How could we forget good ol' Kokoro?" Michael said sarcastically. "In fact, why *didn't* you tell me about him?"

"When I mentioned Kokoro before, you thought me insane," Sumio said. "I felt that if I said anything about him again you would have me placed in a hospital or jail, destroying all hope of stopping him."

"So, why tell us now?" Michael asked.

"What difference does it make? I am already under arrest. Now I can only hope to find some peace within my true self in knowing that I tried to warn you."

"Thanks Sumio, I'll keep that in mind. Meanwhile we'll see to it that several doctors get a good look at you before court."

"Will you do me a favor, please?" Sumio asked. "I mean, really do me a favor?"

"What is it?"

"I know that somewhere beneath that narrow mind of yours and those eyes, blinded by routine, and that sarcastic tongue, there is a very intelligent man. A very good cop. Will you please take time to yourself soon and think over everything that has happened? I know that if you do, you will see the truth and come to me for help, instead of prosecution."

"Don't worry, I'll be thinking everything over, Sumio."

"You will need my help."

"I can handle it myself, thank you."

"I'll be waiting."

"Fine."

Michael nodded to Randy, who again gently started moving Sumio towards and through the office door. Their footsteps faded down the hallway.

"You look like you're a thousand miles away," Facts said, noticing the distant gaze on his partner's face. "What 'cha think'n about?"

"Aw, nothing," Michael said, walking back to his desk with his hands in his pockets. He stood and looked out the window over the lights of the city.

"Yo! What's this dopey stuff?" Facts said. "Cheer up, guy. You just solved another one, hands down. Your record is still flawless."

"Yeah," Michael said, still looking out the window. "Ya wanna do me a favor?"

"I know. Shut the fuck up and leave you alone," Facts said.

Michael laughed. "No," he said, turning around and picking up the square plastic case, "I'm talking about this. Can you check it out for me?"

"I'll see what I can do," Facts said, taking the computer disk and looking it over.

"If you can," Michael said, "find out what that is, where it came from, and if anybody is looking for it."

"OK," Facts said as he started for the hall. "First, I'm

gonna grab a sandwich," he mumbled mostly to himself. "Ya want one?"

Michael shook his head. "No thanks. I've got a couple hours worth of paper to deal with yet."

"OK, it's your stomach."

"I'm all right. I don't like eating too late."

"Whatever you say. It won't make *MY* stomach growl," Facts said picking at an imaginary something on the office door frame. "Ya know, Michael," he hesitantly started saying, "I've been with you a lot of times when you closed a case and put a guy away for murder."

"Yeah, you have," Michael said, turning from the window. "More times than a person can remember."

"Eighty-three," Facts said quietly. "Eighty-four, counting this one."

"Well, I guess I meant most people."

Both men were quiet for an uncomfortably long minute. Michael, with his hat tipped back, one hand in his pocket, stood and thoughtlessly tapped a ballpoint pen on the edge of a paperweight at his desk. Facts continued to pick at the door frame.

A flicker of lightning silhouetted the buildings across the busy street. The night sky outside grew as bright as noon for just an instant, then black again.

"Something I always notice about you," Facts continued, "is that you're like a little kid. Every time you close a case and lock up a bad guy, you get this look in your eyes. Like a sparkle ... like a victory sparkle."

"Get outta here, really?" Michael looked embarrassed.

"Yeah, no shit."

"I never realized."

"Yeah, it's there. Every time."

The muffled rumble of thunder shook the walls of the old building.

"Yeah," Facts said. "Eighty-four homicide arrests and I've seen that victory sparkle every time ... except tonight."

The smile faded from Michael's face and the tapping of the pen increased.

"What's going on here, dude?" Facts asked his partner. "I definitely don't like these gloomy vibes I'm getting from you, pal."

"I don't know," Michael spun and shoved his hands deep into his pockets.

"I just don't know," he repeated, looking out the window.

"You've got more evidence against this guy than two-thirds of your other cases. You've got 'im, hands down. Michael, what's the problem?"

There was no response.

"What more could you want besides a confession? You probably won't get it, but we already know Tanaka's nuts."

The silence continued.

Facts watched his partner for a few more seconds then started down the hall.

"Fine! ... Just fine!" he said over his shoulder. "I can take a hint. I'll come back later after you've had a nap." The frustrated detective mumbled a selection of four letter words as he trotted to catch the elevator.

Michael stood alone in the deserted office. He still gazed out the window. The lights from the streets and neon signs began to blur as large droplets of rain thumped against the thick plate glass.

"Damn!" Michael said under his breath.

What was this feeling he had?

"Damn."

ELEVEN

"You did what?" The look of disbelief covered Bonita's face. She glared down at Michael sitting at his desk.

"I let him go," Michael said quietly. "I'll explain more later."

"Later! No sir, Mr. Finder, you explain right now! How could you let Sumio Tanaka go? He's a murderer."

"It's just not that simple."

"Michael, I was so relieved when you told me you arrested him. You even said you had tons of evidence against him. What happened to all that?"

"Bo, you don't understand."

"Did some big shot tell you to drop the case? Are you going to let him go out and kill some more people?"

"Bo, I ..."

"The man's a living chop-o-matic! Slicing and dicing his way through the city. You finally arrest him, and then what? You let him go!"

"Look Bo, I've been in the deputy prosecutor's office all morning. I've got my reasons for what I've done."

"Well I hope you can explain your reasons to the family of the next victim." Bonita started to storm out of the office, then stopped herself. She slowly turned to face Michael and heaved a deep sigh. "I'm sorry. I get so scared and frustrated. My temper goes haywire and I make a total ass of myself. I...I know you know what you're doing."

Michael smiled. "Everything will be all right," he said. "I do know what I'm doing."

"I certainly hope so," the green-eyed woman said, smiling back. "You know, you're scaring me with some of your police tactics."

"What can I say?" Michael mused. He noticed a deep green sweater draped across Bonita's left arm. "Where in the world are you going with a sweater on a hot day like today?" Michael pointed with his pen as he asked.

"Oh ..." Bonita giggled. "I suppose this does look a little silly, but I'm going over to the museum in a bit. The air-conditioning over there is freezing."

"What's going on at the museum?"

"Nothing special. I've been going in to help out with some typing and filing. Plus, I'll go crazy if I don't keep busy."

"I'm sorry I'm holding you up from your work."

"I'm in no hurry to leave Indianapolis now." She winked. "Come on over later and I'll buy you lunch. Maybe that will help make up for all of the fussin' I've been doing."

"You're on. I'll be over around 1:00."

Bonita waved as she left.

"Hi, Bonita," Michael could hear Facts saying in the hall. "Did I hear someone mention lunch?"

The clack of her high heels drowned her answer, but whatever it was, it made both Bo and Facts laugh. Facts was still laughing when he walked into the office. Beside him stood a gruff-looking man in a military dress uniform. The crisp jacket of the uniform was covered with all sorts of medals and pins. His rough features looked as if they had been exposed to the weather for their entire forty-eight years. The short sun-bleached hairs on his scalp were barely visible even at their lowest point. A chicken-claw-shaped scar on the soldier's right cheek seemed to hold a story within itself.

"Michael, I'd like you to meet Major Stanley Hamilton from the Army," Facts began the introduction. "He's the man that responded to my request for info on the computer disk."

"Major Hamilton," Michael said, standing and firmly shaking the officer's hand.

The men exchanged normal greetings and gathered around the detective's desk with coffee mugs, folders and photos from hours of investigation.

"When that disk was taken," Major Hamilton said, "eleven men were killed at Stockford. All of them pretty much the same way your people here were killed."

"I never heard anything about the murders at Stockford," Michael said.

"And you probably won't hear any more than what I tell you. In fact, Michael ... May I call you Mike?"

"I prefer Michael, but you can call me anything you like."

"You'll get along a lot better if ya just stick to Michael," Facts said, taking a sip of coffee.

"OK ... Michael it is," the major agreed. He took off his jacket and hung it over the back of his chair. "All right gentlemen," he continued, "nothing that we discuss can leave this room. The incident at Stockford has a lot of classified information involved, but I realize we're going to have to work together on this."

"I'm all for that." Michael tipped his hat back and sat up. "Tell us about your deal at the base, Stanley ... Uh, may I call you Stanley?"

"You can call me anything you want," the rugged officer said smiling, "but if you don't call me Stan, I'll start howling at the moon and piss my pants."

The three men laughed. The little joke served as a great ice breaker for what could have been the beginning of a very starched session.

"Stan it is," Michael said. He tapped his diet cola can against the major's coffee cup in a simple toast to their humorous agreement.

In the next hour, Stan Hamilton went over the gruesome details of the murder scene at Stockford. Facts and Michael listened intensely as the officer's macabre story unfolded.

Facts finally spoke. "So ... are you saying Tanaka's your man?" he asked.

"Well, you would think so at first," Stan said, "but after talking to his lawyer this morning and some people that were with Tanaka, the man has an alibi as solid as a brick wall. He was at a dinner with the Governor's League the night of our attack. There must have been over a hundred people that saw him."

"What about your computer disk?" Michael asked. "What's on that anyway?"

"Well, that's another point that doesn't figure out," Stan said. "Although the information on the disk is classified, it's not anything to kill for. Just a usage index for all of the satellites we monitor. Most of that stuff isn't that hard to find on the Net."

"Well, there's no doubt that Tanaka's involved somehow ... After all, the disk was with the jade dragon. That, we know, Tanaka was interested in. It turned up at his house with some dead thugs. He may not tell us everything, but we've got him smothered with circumstantial evidence," Michael said.

"If that's the case, why the hell did you let him go?" Stan asked.

"I've got a plan."

"Well I hope it's a damned good one. You mind letting me in on your little plan?"

"I can't right now, Stan. I'm sorry."

"I thought we were going to work together on this."

Michael lifted his hat completely from his head about three inches, allowing the warm steaming air inside to escape, then dropped it back down and nestled it in place. "You're right," he said. "Here's the way I see it. Those goons at Tanaka's weren't interested in computer software for satellites. That's a higher class of trade than those guys have ever seen. I think someone sent them as heavies to make the payoff."

"Who do you think that is?" Stan asked.

"I don't know, but we've got everything they could possibly want. We have the disk, the jade dragon, the money, and the men they used are dead. Somebody has been ripped off, so-to-speak. Probably whoever this somebody is, they're pissed off and just waiting to have a little chat with Sumio Tanaka."

"We've made sure the news media is spreading the word on Tanaka's release," Facts said.

Major Hamilton nodded his head. "OK, I see," he said. "You keep an eye on Tanaka and when the mystery people try to get him, we get them."

"Hopefully," Michael added. "It's risky, but we need to take the chance. I feel like there's more to this. If we can find this other person, or persons, it will, more than likely, answer a lot of questions for us and for you."

"Yeah," Stan said. "Like why someone would kill so many people and pay so much money for some worthless information and a jade sculpture."

A large black detective in a brown suit jacket leaned in the office door. He was frantically trying to tie a tie around his neck. "There you are!" he said, in his baritone voice.

"Hey Bobby, what's up?" Michael said.

"Man, they've been trying to get hold of you on the radio. I'm on my way up to court and thought I'd check here."

"I've been in a meeting and had my radio turned down. What's up?"

"I'm not sure, but I think they've got another one at the art museum. A woman this time. Someone you know or something like that."

"Who?!" Michael shouted, his voice stressed.

"I don't know, but they wanted you."

Michael felt sick! He had a churning knot in the pit of his stomach. Grabbing his police radio from the desk, he started for his car.

"Yo, Michael!" Facts said, putting his hand across his partner's chest. "Hey man, don't go. I'll handle this. You don't need to see that."

"I'll be all right," Michael said and charged out the door.

"Damn him!" Facts slammed his fist into a file cabinet. "He's so fucking hardheaded. C'mon Major, we can still get there before him."

Bewildered, Stan Hamilton yanked his jacket from the back of his chair and followed the chubby detective. "What's going on?" he asked as they entered the stairwell instead of waiting for the elevator.

"We still have a chance to get there before Michael," Facts said. "His car's in the parking garage. Mine's out front."

"So, why do we need to get there first?" the major asked, swinging across a landing and starting down another flight of steps.

"The victim ..." Facts explained as both men burst out a first-level exit door, "is probably Bo Baker. Michael's been kinda dating her for a couple of weeks. I don't want him to freak out on me. Things are tough enough in this world without having to see someone you care about with their head cut off."

"Now I'm with you," Major Hamilton said.

Even driving the wildest he had driven since his rookie days, Facts and the major still only managed to arrive at the museum seconds before Michael. Several marked police cruisers were parked haphazardly in the chaotic parking lot. Some still had their red lights flashing. News reporters and curious pedestrians lined a strip of yellow crime scene tape that stretched from trees and bushes blocking the entrance to the art museum.

Facts, along with Stan Hamilton, ducked under the crime tape and tried to catch up with Michael who had already made it half way up the front steps. The gray-haired uniform sergeant that was at the scene of the previous murders stood atop the stone steps.

"Topper!" Facts shouted, pointing at Michael. "Stop him. It's a friend of his!"

The elderly sergeant gripped Michael by his shoulders as he started by. "Easy Michael," he said softly. "I'm sorry, Son, I had no idea it was someone you knew that well. I never would have called if I'd known. Why don't you let Facts handle this one?"

"I'm OK, Topper," Michael said. "We just went out a few times over the last couple of weeks. Really, I'm all right."

Facts stepped beside his partner, out of breath from climbing the steps faster than he was accustomed. "Michael, please!" he huffed. "Why do you want to do this?"

"Guys, come on, get outta here. I'm just upset because I knew and liked her. Come on and go with me if it will make you feel better."

All four men surrendered to the compromise and entered

the huge glass doors into the lobby. Topper led the detectives and the major to the office where Michael first met Bonita.

"Geez," Facts quietly hissed as they walked in the room.

"Oh good lord!" Major Hamilton said.

Michael was silent as they looked over the blood-washed walls and venetian blinds behind the desk. A woman's head, the hair saturated with crimson fluid, sat hideously in the leather desk chair. The body was lying between the chair and the desk, completely bathed in blood. Almost unrecognizable, a green sweater lay stained and wet on the office floor.

"You sure you want to do this?" Facts asked placing his palm gently against Michael's back.

"Yeah," he said, slowly nodding. "Go ahead an' start crime lab."

"Anything ya need, Michael, let me know," Topper said. "You gonna be OK?"

"Yeah, thanks Top. I just feel a little bad. If I hadn't taken so long to clear this up, she'd be back in Japan alive and happy."

"Japan?" Topper scratched his head. "Why was she going to Japan?"

"That's where she lives."

"Wait a minute," Topper said, pulling his note book from his pants pocket. "Who are we talking about here?"

"Her," Michael said pointing to the corpse. "Bonita Baker."

"Bonita Baker?" the uniform sergeant said, looking over his notes. "That's the girl that called this in. She's down the hall in another office. Pretty shook up, from what I understand. This girl here is ..."

"Michael!" A woman's voice called from the lobby. A familiar voice, music to the stressed detective's ears. Facts and Stan parted as Michael passed between them and through the door. Bonita stood with her arms out. Tears were streaming down her cheeks.

"Oh Michael!" she cried. "Did you see what he did to Connie?" Her words were almost inaudible as she shook uncontrollably from crying.

Michael swept Bo up in a ferocious hug. They embraced silently for several seconds, then Michael spoke.

"I thought it was you," he whispered.

"No, it's Connie."

"Your sweater, it threw me off."

"Connie was cold. She forgot hers, so I let her borrow mine while I went to make some coffee. It's not as cold in the break room. When I came back ..." Bonita began to sob and buried her face in Michael's shoulder.

"This is it," Michael said, easing Bo away. "The museum is closed until I find out what's going on. I don't want anyone else hurt during this investigation."

"I begged you not to let him go," Bonita said. "I told you what would happen. Now look."

Michael turned to Facts.

"Did you make that call for me, partner?"

"Sure did."

"Are they here yet?"

"Right outside. Are you satisfied?"

"Yeah. Call 'em in."

Facts went across the lobby and out the huge glass doors of the art museum.

"Michael, what's going on?" Bonita said as the doors closed behind Facts.

Stan Hamilton had remained quiet as long as possible.

"Detective Finder, would you mind telling me what the hell is going on here?"

"Hold on everybody. Give me a chance," Michael said.

After about two minutes one of the museum doors swung open. Facts was holding it wide and stepping out of the way. In walked Sumio Tanaka, followed by a corrections officer from the county jail. Sumio's wrists were handcuffed behind his back.

"What's he doing here!" Bonita screamed and grabbed Michael's arm.

"It's all right," Michael assured her.

"Here, let me get those off of you," Facts said, unlocking and removing Sumio's handcuffs.

"I hope you haven't been too uncomfortable," Michael said to him.

"I adjust well," Sumio said, rubbing his wrist where the steel cuffs had creased the skin.

"I never meant for anything like this to happen, but, nonetheless, I suppose it clears you."

"I've heard another has been slain."

Michael nodded toward the office where Connie's body was.

"May I?" Sumio asked.

"Just don't touch anything, please," Michael said.

With no expression on his face, hands relaxed at his sides, Sumio slowly analyzed the gory scene.

"What's he doing here?" Bo whispered again.

"Yes, Michael, what *is* he doing here?" Stan Hamilton asked in much less of a whisper than Bo.

Michael tipped his hat back and stuck his hands in his pockets. "Mr. Tanaka didn't kill Connie, or Tiller and the guard for that matter," he said.

"How can you say that?" Bo asked louder. "Especially now, after what's happened today."

"I know he didn't kill them," Michael said. "Sumio's been in jail since night before last."

"Sure but you let him out early this morning," Bo said. "Apparently that was all the time he needed."

"I never let him out," Michael said smiling.

Bonita's green eyes widened and her mouth dropped open.

Major Hamilton shook his head. "You mean the whole time the newspapers and television were reporting his release, Tanaka was sitting locked up in your county jail?" he asked.

"That's exactly where he's been."

"Why you son-of-a-bitch!" The major said. "You lied to me!"

"Sorry again," Michael said. "The fewer people that knew

what was happening, the better I could trust the results of my little test. I thought they would go for Sumio though. I've got people watching his house. I really didn't think they would hurt anyone else." Michael looked at the tearful Bonita and gave her another gentle hug. "I'm sorry this happened," he said softly in her ear.

"So, where are you now in this investigation?" the major asked. "I see what has happened, but what does it all mean?"

"I guess it means, back to the drawing board," Michael said. "Someone is trying desperately to frame Sumio. I don't know who or why."

"The who ... is Mizu Kokoro," Sumio said. He had quietly returned from viewing the crime scene. "The why ... is because I am the only one who has a chance at stopping him."

"Who the hell is Miss Koo-Koo?" Major Hamilton asked.

"I'll tell you later," Michael said trying to brush the question by.

"No ... Now, damn it!" Stan Hamilton put his hands on his hips. "I've only known you for a few hours and you've already lied and withheld information from me. This is not what I call cooperating."

"I'll tell you all about it when we get back to the office Stan, I promise."

"Officer!" the frustrated major called out to one of the uniformed policemen. "Where's a phone around here I can use, please?"

"Oh, no," Michael moaned and looked at Facts. "See if you can calm him down for me ... would ya?"

"I'll see what I can do," Facts said, following down a hall where the major had rushed out of sight.

"May I say something without your throwing me back in jail?" Sumio asked.

Michael took a deep breath and let it out.

"What is it, Sumio?" he said.

"The brutal murder that has occurred in the other room is not the work of Kokoro."

"It's not?"

"No. You probably could not tell the difference, but I can."

"How can you tell? What's different?"

"Years of training," Sumio said. "This is perhaps a student of Fushigi Sh'Kata, but not Kokoro."

"Shit! That certainly adds a twist to everything," Michael said.

"What are we going to do now?" Sumio asked.

"*We* are not doing anything," Michael said. "However, *I* have another plan."

TWELVE

"You don't have to do this if you don't want to," Michael said looking into Bonita's eyes. He was trying to determine just how affected she was by what they were starting.

"No, I'm OK," Bonita said, even though she was wiping a tear from her cheek. "Just don't leave me."

"I won't leave you. We'll get this over with as soon as possible. I can't help but think that maybe these murders have been committed to scare people away from the museum. There must be something in here that they want us to stay away from. They must have known I would close everything down."

"What good will an inventory of the art collection do?"

"I'm not sure. I think that as much as this collection travels around, it would be a great opportunity to smuggle drugs from one place to another. Especially now that everything is headed out of the country."

Michael reached and tore the paper coroner's seal that was stuck across the two glass doors into the museum. Bonita handed the key to the detective and shuddered.

"It's OK," Michael said, unlocking the huge doors. "They've cleaned up everything."

"Still, I don't want to go into the office. The folders we need are in the top drawer of the gray file cabinet."

Michael retrieved the necessary records and, along with Bonita, went to the third floor where stacks of crates and boxes awaited their journey back to Japan. The freshly washed and waxed floor of the area leading into the storage room showed no signs of the slayings that had sparked the puzzling investigation.

Bonita rubbed the goose bumps from her arms while they passed over the spot where Clevous Tiller's body had been. She looked over the area and shook her head. Her eyes darted to the far wall where the young guard's detached head had rested.

"I guess they do a pretty good job at cleaning up things like this," Bonita said quietly.

Michael put his arm around her and guided her into the room with the stored art pieces. "Let's get our minds on this," he said. "How about this one?" Michael squatted beside the closest box.

"What's the number on it?"

"Let's see ... two, two-seven, four."

Bonita ran her pen down the series of numbers on the sheet clipped to the clipboard. "That's Buta, the emperor's swine, in ivory."

Using a hammer to tap a small pry bar under the lid, Michael began to work the top off of the hat-box-sized crate. "Yep ... it's an ivory pig all right," he said, crudely tacking the lid back down.

"Next." Bonita checked that item off then poised her pen over the list preparing to scan for the next number.

After three hours partially opened cases were scattered all about the disorganized room. Somewhere near the back of the jumbled stack, Michael could be heard thumping and bumping around. Bonita sat on one of the boxes that had been shoved against the wall. The wall served as a useful backrest. She stretched and yawned, arching her back to chase the stiffness that had set in.

"Can we take a break?" she asked toward the rustling in the back of the room.

"Yeah, hold on, Bo," a voice answered back. "This one's as tall as you and me. What's in two, one-nine, one?"

Bonita finished her stretch, then focused on the list once again.

"That's bamboo armor worn by samurai soldiers."

Tap ... tap ... tap. Creeaak!

"Right again." Michael's voice was muffled. "How many more do we have to go?"

Bonita sighed. "I don't know," she said, glancing over the list. "A lot."

"OK, OK, I'm coming out."

"Good, I'm starving."

After a few seconds, Michael's voice didn't sound any closer. "Hey, Bo?" he said.

"What, Michael?" Bonita was sitting with her face in her hands, slowly massaging her tired eyes.

"What's in this big crate back here against the wall?"

"What's the number?"

"I can't find one. I think it's the biggest one back here."

"The largest case we have would be the drums, and you've already opened that one."

"No ... I remember the drums. This one is much bigger than that."

Tap ... tap ... tap ... tap, creak. Tap ... tap ... creak.

Bonita began to maneuver her way around and over opened cases toward the back of the room where Michael was. He was prying at the side of a case that was about five feet tall, fifteen feet long and five feet thick. Michael had draped his tie and suit jacket over one of the boxes.

"You really don't take off your hat, do you?" Bonita said, walking up on Michael as he pried at the side of the large crate.

"What *is* this?" Michael asked, ignoring her comment.

"I've never seen this one before," Bo said. "It might not be ours."

Michael grunted and tugged as the side panel popped loose. Bonita jumped back when the heavy wood cover fell away, causing a loud crash.

"What is it?" Bonita asked, creeping closer.

"A machine or something," Michael said, looking over the large cylindrical contraption. "Uh oh! Wait a minute," the detective said, shining a flashlight along some wires that led to a bundle of what looked like dynamite. The red, white, black and green wires ran from the cylinder to one end of the wrapped sticks of explosives, then to a square box with tiny yellow lights. A white dish-like piece three feet in diameter sat on top of the square control box facing upward. There were several other wires and cables running between the box and the large cylinder.

Bonita eased nearer to Michael and took hold of his left

arm, cautiously positioning herself slightly behind the policeman's shoulder. "Is it a bomb?" she asked.

"I'd say that would be a good guess," Michael said, reaching for his jacket and tie.

"What are you doing?" the wide-eyed Bo asked.

"The same thing you're getting ready to do ... Get the fuck out of here. I'm going to get the bomb squad. Let's get to a phone."

"Why don't you use your radio?" she asked nervously.

"Radio transmissions can detonate some types of explosives. I'm not in the mood to find out if this is one of those."

"Michael, I'm scared. What's a bomb doing here?"

"I don't know. Let's discuss this while we're getting our asses outta here." He pushed Bonita toward the exit.

"I want you away from here," Michael said once they were outside in the circular drive.

"What do you mean?"

"I want you to get back to your hotel room. You'll be safe there."

"No! I want to stay with you."

"You can't, Bo. I'm going to be tied up here for a bit. I'm not sure what this all means. Go back to the hotel and lock yourself in your room. Don't open the door for anyone. Anyone! You got that?" He took her face in his hands and gently kissed her lips.

"Will you call and check on me? I'm scared," Bonita said.

"I'll call as soon as I get done here, I promise."

"Don't forget!"

"I won't."

Michael watched as Bonita folded her shapely figure into her rented black Toyota. "Don't stop anywhere!" he shouted as she drove by and waved.

Even with a city the size of Indianapolis, there just wasn't a great need for a bomb squad. Michael could think of only two other times in the last few years when the squad had been used. Understandably, the explosives van took about forty minutes to arrive, but once on the scene, the three team members quickly donned their protective padding and entered the deserted museum. Michael paced nervously behind the open doors of the unmarked bomb squad van.

"What's taking them so long?" he said into the back of the van. "They've been in there for almost an hour."

"I don't know. Why don't you run in there and ask 'em?" Facts' voice came from inside the van. The detective sat in a folding chair in the center of the van. The early evening light reflected in his round glasses as he read a thick manual taken from a shelf near his seat.

"No, thanks." Michael paced in front of the doors and stopped. "What the hell are you doing in there?" he asked, looking up into the van.

"This is fascinating," Facts said, peering from the manual. "The number of ways people think of how to blow things up. This book is full of different kinds of bombs, and how to defuse them."

"You planning on transferring to the bomb squad?"

"Shit, no! Working with you is all the proof I'm going to

give them that I'm crazy."

Michael smiled and started to comment, but his attention was drawn toward the museum entrance.

A heavily padded bomb squad member emerged from the glass doors of the building. His brown hair was matted with sweat. He removed some pads and set them at Facts' feet in the van. His police shirt was soaking wet.

"What've you got, Cookie?" Michael anxiously asked. "Is everything OK?"

"Now it is," the bomb expert said, lighting up a cigarette. He leaned into the van and looked along the row of books and manuals that were lined on the floor.

"Well ... tell me something," Michael said.

"Hang on a second." The technician took another drag from his cigarette and scanned along the row of books again.

"You lookin' for this?" Facts asked, holding up the manual he had been reading.

"Yeah, there it is," the policeman said. He took the manual, flipped through some pages, and scribbled some notes in the margin.

"Cookie?" Michael said impatiently.

"Hang on." More notes were scribbled. "There." Cookie finally said and handed the manual back to Facts. "Sorry, Michael. I had to jot some things down while they were still fresh in my mind."

"OK, now tell me!"

"All right, all right." Cookie took the cigarette from his

mouth and blew the smoke out to the side. "Whoever put that son-of-a-bitch in there knew exactly what they were doing," he said. "You know, I've never had a nuclear bomb before."

"Nuclear?" Michael shouted. "Get outta here!"

"Yeah, and not just some high school project, either. That big mother could have leveled the whole city."

Facts sat with his mouth open. His face was pale.

"You have got to be shittin' me," he said.

"Now, I think you've got some terrorists on your hands, and they must be some of those crazy sons-of-bitches too."

"Why'd you say that?" Michael asked.

"Well ... this thing was set up to be detonated by remote control. Even with a strong transmitter, you couldn't set it off without blowin' yourself up. Either they're stupider than shit or they're those suicide guys that aren't afraid of dying for a cause."

"You have got to be shittin' me," Facts mumbled again.

"Wait a minute!" Michael said. "I thought I saw dynamite in that crate."

"You did."

"Since when did they start using dynamite in nuclear bombs?"

"They haven't," Cookie explained. "That's what was taking us so long. The nuclear bomb was easy to figure out. Whoever set this up hooked in an anti-tamper system with the dynamite. Now *that* mother was the best I've ever seen. That's what I was writing those notes about. If you didn't make just the right moves and cut the right wires, ka-plowee!"

"I'm glad you know what you're doing." Michael patted the officer on his back.

"Well, I'll tell ya," Cookie said, lighting the end of a fresh cigarette with the butt of his old one. "It looked like a basic hook-up that I'm pretty familiar with. But just when I was fixin' to clip a wire, I noticed an extra wire that changed everything. By the way," he added, "if you had pried off the top of that crate instead of the side, I'd have to be telling you all this through a spiritualist by now."

"I don't even want to think about it. Can we turn our radios on?"

"Yeah, Sky and Tinker are checking things out before we move it. We'll be able to tell you a lot more about it probably tomorrow sometime."

Michael removed his radio from under his suit jacket and turned it on. "47-57, control," he said into the radio.

"Go ahead, sir," a woman's voice answered.

"Everything's clear here at the art museum. We'll have our radios back on."

"OK, sir, stand by. I think someone was trying to contact you."

Michael held the radio up and listened.

Cookie had gathered some equipment and had already started inside the building.

"You've *got* to be shitting me!" Facts was still sitting in the back of the bomb van, clutching the manual.

"Come on, Facts, get over it," Michael said. "It's safe now, turn your radio on."

The stunned detective mechanically reached over and picked up his radio from a fold-down shelf. With a twist of the silver button on top, his radio clicked back to life. "A fucking nuclear bomb," he said. "What are we supposed to do with a nuclear bomb? What are we supposed to do?"

Before Michael could answer, a gruff voice came over his police radio.

"Car One to 47-57," it barked.

"Car One?" Michael said to his partner. "That's the chief. What the hell does he want?"

"Yo! He probably wants to know what you're going to do with this fucking nuclear bomb you found!" Facts blurted. "Come to think of it ..."

Michael held up his hand to his chattering partner and pushed the button on the side of his radio. "47-57, go ahead Chief."

"Are you familiar with Major Stan Hamilton from the United States Army?"

"Yes, sir, I've met the Major." Michael shrugged his shoulders at Facts, still uncertain where the chief's message was leading.

"He just left my office a little while ago, en route to your location," the gravely voice barked. "I expect full cooperation from you and Detective Brown on this investigation. Do you understand? Full cooperation!"

"Yes, sir," Michael said into the radio. "I understand." He turned the radio down and clipped it onto his belt. "That Major Hamilton. What a whiny-ass baby!" he said.

"Yo, Michael," Facts called to his partner.

"I'm sorry, man, but this really pisses me off," Michael apologized. "What's the Army doing nowadays, training a bunch of pussies to be officers?"

"Yo, Michael."

"You know it's bad enough we've got these murders, and now this bomb. But now we've got to baby-sit a military asshole!"

"Uh ... Michael."

"You know what I would like to do?"

"Michael ... I think ... uhh ..."

"I'd like to take *this* bomb and stuff it up Hamilton's ass and send them *both* back to Washington. That would take care of two of our problems."

"Yooo-whooo, Michael," Facts tried to quickly shake his head.

"What?" Michael said, finally noticing the slight, but desperate, gestures of his partner. Facts was looking just over Michael's shoulder. Spinning around, Michael's face came within inches of the scar-faced man standing immediately behind him. "Ahh ... Major Hamilton!" The startled Detective Finder forced a smile. "What a pleasant surprise. We were just talking about you."

"Knock off the crap, Finder." Major Hamilton's voice was as sober as the chief's.

"Have you and the chief been drinking out of the same cup?" Michael asked.

"Save it, Finder!" The major was practically gritting his teeth. "I've worked with people who didn't like me before. I can deal with that. But I've got eleven dead men that were probably killed by the same person committing the murders in your city, and I'm going to find out who he is -- whether you like it or not. You have your orders. No more little plans without me. Got it?"

"I suppose you and your little Army stations haven't kept any secrets?"

"I assure you, what goes on in those bases is strictly in the nation's best interest!"

"What I do during my investigation is in the best interest of the citizens of Indianapolis! Not the United States Army!"

"I had hoped it wouldn't come to this, Michael, but I'm reminding you of your orders. What's it going to be?"

Michael shoved his hands into his pockets and spun away from the major. He kicked at a balled up potato chip bag that had accidentally tumbled out of the bomb van from where Facts was sitting. "What do you want to know?" Michael said, looking at the museum and trying to calm his temper.

"For starters," Major Hamilton said, "what were you doing here this afternoon?"

Michael turned back to face the soldier. "I thought that maybe the killer was trying to scare people away from the art cases to protect something hidden in them."

"Something like what?"

"Well ... like drugs, or weapons. I don't know ... maybe some of your military secrets."

Facts climbed down from the van and picked up the crumpled potato chip bag at Michael's feet. "Or a nuclear bomb," he said as he passed the major on the way to a large trash can a few feet away.

"What?!" the major gasped, momentarily losing his composure. "*Nuclear*?!"

"That's right," Michael said. "A big one. Now you know what I know."

"Did you tell your chief about this?"

"As a matter-of-fact," Michael said, adjusting his hat. "No I haven't. I just need a little time to think before I start trying to explain all of this to other people."

"Well ..." Major Hamilton said thoughtfully. "I guess that simplifies everything."

"How so?"

"Well ... stolen military information in the same investigation with a nuclear bomb pretty well takes matters out of your hands, doesn't it?"

"Get outta here," Michael said. "No way, Stan. What makes you think you're taking this assignment from me?"

"Michael, let's face it. Stolen Army software and nuclear bombs are best left alone by a local police department. Besides, I have a few ideas myself. You're not the only one that can think around here, you know."

"What kind of ideas are you talking about?"

"This bomb just confirms what I've been working on."

"What's that?"

"Terrorists."

"Why terrorists?"

"Well ... they get the military's attention by killing eleven men and taking classified software. Then, they try to get the public's attention by killing Tanaka. Uh ... trying to kill Tanaka. I guess they didn't figure on how good he was with that Kung-fu stuff."

"Fushigi Sh'Kata," Facts said. He had returned from his trip to the trash can and was now sitting on the back of the bomb van.

"Yeah, whatever," the major said. "Anyway, terrorists love attention. That's how they get their issues exposed to the world."

"What about this bomb? How does that fit in?" Michael asked.

"That's the interesting part," the major said. "Listen up. All through history, captives were taken in exchange for release of political prisoners or financial gain."

"I'm listening."

"Well, it seldom works anymore. Most governments have developed policies that forbid dealing with terrorists under any circumstances."

"So?"

"So, why not find one of the wealthiest men in the world, like Masato Kudo, and hold one of his most treasured possessions for ransom?"

"Like his art collection."

Major Hamilton smacked his fist into his palm. "Right!" he shouted. "Kudo's worth billions. He can afford a few million to keep his multi-million dollar art collection from being blown up."

"Sounds great, Stan, but why a nuclear bomb? The anti-tamper bomb they had hooked up was enough to level the whole building and everything in it."

"Now we're back to the attention, again. If Kudo refuses, a bomb is worldwide attention toward their demands."

"Stan, I ... I ... I don't know what to say. I never thought of all that. As much as I don't want to admit it, that's a great concept."

A smug little smile spread across the Army officer's face. "I know a few things," he said.

"Jeez! Working with you has taught me a lot," Michael lied. "I'm sorry if I've been a pain in the ass."

"Oh, I understand," Major Hamilton said. He put his arm over Michael's shoulder. "You just got in over your head on this."

"You're probably right ... Do you still think I should turn everything over to you?"

"I think it would be best, don't you?" Hamilton was beginning to sound fatherly.

"Yeah, you seem to be more qualified to handle this," Michael said.

"Well, now," Hamilton chuckled. "I don't know about all that ... but, fine. I'll square everything away with your chief."

"Uhh ... Michael, can I talk with you for a minute?" Facts said, waving his index finger.

Michael simultaneously interrupted and ignored Facts. "Yeah, uh ... Stan," he said. "You're probably going to want all of our notes on this case, aren't you?"

"That would be helpful."

"Well ... do you mind if we have a day to gather up everything and get it organized? I mean, I've got notes at home and all over my desk at the office. I was in Facts' den this morning and ... Oh, you should see the mess. Notes and pages everywhere!"

Facts was baffled. "What are you talking about?" he said. "You know I don't take notes." The puzzled detective then noticed the stern look on his partner's face. "Ohh! ..." Facts said. "You mean the notes on these murders we've had here lately. Yeah ... oh yeah, tons of notes all over the place. I thought he meant something else."

"We can get it all together in a day, can't we?" Michael asked.

"Oh, sure," Facts said. "We'll have everything ready tomorrow."

Michael frowned from behind Stan and rapidly shook his head.

"Yo ... uh ... I don't mean tomorrow. I meant the ... day after," Facts said.

Michael nodded in agreement with the change.

"That'll be fine," Stan said. "Quite frankly, I didn't think you guys would go along with all this without a fight. It'll take a day for me to get all of my people up here anyway."

"I'm kinda glad you're takin' this off my hands," Michael said.

"You've done a good job. I'll set things straight with your boss." The major excused himself and returned to his car to look for some forms.

Michael stepped over beside his partner.

"OK," Facts whispered. "There's two things I'm sure of. One, you would never turn a case over to an asshole like Hamilton, orders or no orders. Two, you know damn well I haven't written a note my entire career. What are you up to?"

"Maybe now, if he thinks he's on the case, it will keep him busy enough to stay out of our way."

"What's going to happen in two days when he wants all those notes and files we don't have?"

"I don't know. I'll worry about that when he asks for them. In the meantime, we've got a couple days to work this out."

"What do you think about this bomb? Any ideas?"

"I'm not sure, but you can bet your ass it's not terrorists. I'm also pretty sure that Tiller and the guard didn't get killed because they stumbled across a burglary here the other night."

"What then?"

"I don't think they got killed by anyone taking stuff out. I think they caught someone bringing something in. Namely, this bomb. Whoever killed them staged the burglary to cover their real motive."

"Yo ... And when we didn't close the museum down after the first murders, it must have made them nervous, so they killed Bo's friend Connie to add an extra scare."

"Yeah," Michael said. "They got the results they wanted, but they didn't count on my checking all of the crates and finding the bomb."

"That son-of-a-bitch bomb must have been a key part of their plans. I wonder what they're going to do now that it's been discovered."

"I don't know," Michael said quietly.

"Shh ... here he comes."

The major returned from his army-green sedan. He was placing a snub-nose .38 into a shoulder holster concealed beneath his left arm. "There." he said, after slipping his uniform dress jacket back on. "That's better. It's not Army issue, but they can't expect me to run around after some terrorist without a weapon now, can they?"

"You love this, don't you?" Michael said.

Stan smiled and put his hands on his belt. "I'm having fun," he said.

Michael looked at his partner. "You ready to go get a bite to eat?" he asked. "Or is that a stupid question?"

Facts shook out a paper napkin and stuffed it in his collar. "There's no such thing as stupid questions," the detective said. "Didn't you learn anything in high school?"

"My mom doesn't think so ... but I ..."

"Control to 47-57," the voice came through the radio.

"47-57," Michael answered.

"Sir, we've received a message from your office that a Bonita Baker is trying to reach you. They said she sounded upset and left a phone number for you to call. She said she believed someone was after her, and that she had to leave the hotel."

"Ma'am, can you call that number please, and find out where that is, and if Miss Baker needs a squad car there?"

"I already have, sir. It's the number of the Inn-D-Inn on East Washington. She still sounded upset, but she said she just wanted to talk to you."

"Thanks, ma'am. If she calls back, tell her I'm on my way."

"Yes, sir."

Michael clipped the radio onto his belt.

"The Inn-D-Inn?" Facts said. "What a dump. What's she doing there?"

"I don't know," Michael said. "But, will you do me a favor?"

"I know, go to the hotel and find out what's going on there while you check on Bo. Right?"

"Please, man. Let me know on the radio."

"All right," Facts said, "but if everything's OK, I'm going home. It's been a long day."

"I appreciate it. See you tomorrow." Michael ran and jumped into his car and peeled out of the museum's driveway.

"I think this is something I need to look into, also," Major Hamilton said. "Do you mind if I ride with you?"

Facts sighed. "Might as well," he said, pulling the napkin from the front of his shirt. "Hop in. I'll bring you back to your car on my way home."

As Facts started his unmarked police car, he looked up at the entrance to the museum. Cookie was coming out the door, carrying his tool box and the large bundle of dynamite sticks that had hampered the disarming of the larger bomb. Facts turned to the major sitting in the passenger seat beside him. "Stan, can you believe this fucking day?" he said.

"Well," the major said, "until we finish checking out the hotel, I'm not sure this day is over."

THIRTEEN

The Inn-D-Inn was a tattered single-level motel on Indianapolis' near east side. Michael cautiously knocked on the door of unit fourteen. The parking lot in front had a slight stench of urine.

"Who is it?" Bonita's voice answered.

"It's me, Michael. Open up."

The door opened just a crack and one of the blond's teary green eyes peeked out. The door flew all the way open. "Oh Michael!" Bonita shouted. She threw both arms around his neck and gave a powerful hug. "I didn't know what to do. They said you had your radio off. I was ..."

"Hold on, Hon." Michael lifted Bonita up and set her back inside the motel room, closing the door behind him. "Everything's OK. Calm down and tell me who you saw and how you ended up here."

"I don't know. I went to the room at my hotel and changed clothes and had room service bring something to eat. I was being careful like you told me. After I ate a little, I laid across the bed and fell asleep. When I woke up, there was this man!"

"Who, Honey? Who was it?"

"I ... I don't know. I screamed and ... ran for the door. He didn't chase me. He just stood there!"

"How did he get in? Do you know?"

"No. I just got out of there. I tried to call you, but they said your radio was off. I came here and called you again."

"Why'd you come here, Bo? This place is a dump."

"I don't know my way around at all, so I just jumped in a cab and had him drive until I found this place. I just needed sanctuary somewhere. This was the first place I saw."

"Everything will be OK." Michael held the rattled woman with his right hand and operated his police radio with his left. "47-57, to 47-50," he said into the microphone.

"47-50, go ahead," Facts answered.

"Have you found anything over there?"

"No. The manager let us in her room. Everything seems all right. No sign of forced entry. The place hasn't been ransacked or anything, but I don't see her purse."

"I've got that," Bonita said. "I keep it on the doorknob."

"She has her purse," Michael said into the radio. "Thanks for checking it out for me."

"No problem," came the reply. "Is uh ... everything OK over on your end?"

"Everything's fine. I'll get with you in the morning."

"Ten-four."

Michael set his radio down and looked over the musty furnishings. "Well, there's no need for you to stay here," he said. "Let's go over to my place."

"Oh, Michael, let's stay here," Bonita pleaded. "Please, I know it's sleazy, but I don't want to go out anymore tonight. Will you stay with me?"

"I ..."

"Please, Michael."

The detective sighed, turned, and slid the security chain across the door. He twisted the doorknob to double check the lock. "Well ... I suppose," he said.

Bonita slid her arms inside Michael's suit jacket and around his waist. "Good," she cooed, nuzzling her nose into his neck. "I feel much safer."

After drinking diet colas all day, the call of nature had finally lured Michael into the tiny bathroom. With all of the excitement, he hadn't noticed the pressure building in his bladder. "Aahh! Relief!" Michael said aloud.

He flushed, rinsed his hands, and dried them on a gray towel that had most likely been white at one time. "I've seen shitters bigger than that on trains!" Michael said, walking back into the bedroom.

Bonita had slipped into the full-sized bed. The thin blanket and worn sheet were draped seductively over her nakedness. She was beautiful. Michael had forgotten everything he intended to say.

"Are you going to stand there all night?" asked Bonita. "Or, are you going to come be my bodyguard?" She brushed her arm across the space beside her on the bed.

Michael pulled the large chrome .357 handgun from the holster on his belt. He set the weapon on a flimsy nightstand beside the bed with a lamp and an old analog alarm clock. He grabbed the brim of his hat, pulled it off, and tossed it onto a post on the footboard of the bed.

"Well," said Bonita, raising an eyebrow, "I'm honored."

Michael graciously bowed. "Anything to please my mistress," he said.

The policeman stripped quickly. Bonita squealed as Michael dived in on top of her. He pressed against her warmth, pinning her to the bed with the weight of his body. They attacked each others' lips with kisses that only new lovers could produce. The long, steamy kind, that conjure muffled whimpers and moans. Without looking, Michael stretched his hand to the dusty lamp shade, and with a click, plunged the room into darkness. There was a quiet gasp. Then a louder one.

"Uummmm ... Michael!"

Brrrrring!!

Michael jumped. He was torn from deep sleep to somewhere just under half awake. "What ... in the ... hell?" he thought, then slowly started to drift back into tranquillity.

Brrrrring!!

Again, Michael jumped. This time his hand ventured out to frantically find the source of the loud noise. He falsely accused the alarm clock, smacking it across the top, and pushing everything that stuck out the back.

Brrring!!

"Ahh ... !" This had to be it. Michael found the phone on

the second shelf of the nightstand and lifted the receiver. He started back to sleep as his arm dangled over the edge of the bed, still clutching the receiver.

"Hello ... ? Hello ... ? Yo, Michael ..." the faint voice came from the ear piece. "Yo, Michael! Pick up the phone, you dumb-fuck!"

Michael dragged the receiver to his head. It felt like it weighed twenty pounds. In a groggy voice, he said, "Yeah ... what d'ya want?"

"Michael, wake up. It's Facts."

"Facts?" Michael looked at the clock on the nightstand. The background of the face was illuminated in a dim orange yellow light that silhouetted the hands. "It's 3:15, Facts. Are you outta your mind?"

"Sorry, man. I couldn't sleep."

"So you call and wake my ass up. Couldn't this wait?"

"I've got some stuff on my mind. I don't think it's anything big, but it's been bugging me."

"Like what?"

"Well, tonight at the Omni, before I left, I talked to the guy at the front desk. He said he saw Bo leave in a hurry."

"Yeah. She was in a hurry."

"He said she was carrying something long, wrapped in a cloth or something. Do you know what that was?"

Michael sat up on one elbow. "Was that earlier *tonight*?" he asked.

"Yeah, the last time he saw her, when she was probably on her way over there."

"I don't know what that could have been," Michael said.

"There's something else," Facts continued.

"What?" Michael reached his hand out behind him to shake Bonita.

"Remember when I told you I checked on everybody in Japan?" Facts asked.

"Yeah, I'm listening." Michael rolled over, and again ran his hand over the place where Bonita had been. "Shit!" he said. "She's gone!"

"Who, Bo?"

"Yeah ... hold on a second."

After setting the receiver on the bed, Michael swung his feet to the floor. He turned on the lamp. The harsh light made him squint as he quickly scanned the room. The chain was still on the door. The bathroom door was shut with light shining through the space at the bottom. Michael took a deep breath, let it out, then picked up the receiver. "It's OK. She's in the bathroom," he whispered. "Now, what were you saying about checks on everyone in Japan?"

"The people with the art show," Facts continued. "I checked them all."

"And?"

"I checked on Bo."

"What about her?" Michael tensed.

"I couldn't find anything on her."

Michael rubbed his face. "You mean you called me at 3:15 in the morning to tell me you couldn't find anything on Bo!"

"Yo, Michael! Listen to me. I couldn't find *anything*!

Nothing! No one heard of her. Not even at the art museum in Hiroshima."

"Whooaa," Michael said. He turned to glance at the bathroom door again. "Why didn't you tell me this before?"

"I don't know. I guess I didn't want you to think I was checkin' up on your girl behind your back. Plus, I didn't find out about her being unknown in Japan until yesterday. I thought she just didn't show up because she didn't have a criminal record anywhere. I'm sorry, man."

"No ... no Facts, it's OK. You did just what you were supposed to do."

"I did?"

"You bet your ass. Just because I marched off into La-La Land, doesn't mean you should follow. This adds a whole new meaning to some questions I've had myself."

"Like what?"

"Well, the other day when Bo and I were ..." Michael froze. He chopped his sentence off midway and stared at the top of the nightstand.

Facts' faint voice came through the receiver. "Michael, what is it? What's wrong?"

Without answering, Michael set the phone down, dropped to his knees, and wildly began groping under the bed. He ran his hands around the legs of the small table, then under the pillows on the bed. "Shit!"

"Are you all right?" Facts' leprechaun-sounding voice came from somewhere around the bed.

Michael dug the receiver from under the covers and held it to his ear. "My fucking gun is gone!" he said.

"What d'ya mean, gone?"

"I mean gone! Gone, as in, not here! It was right by the bed when I went to sleep."

The toilet flushed.

"I don't like the way this is turning out, man!"

"I'm on my way," Facts said.

"Room fourteen." Michael hung up and reached for his suit pants. He had them on and mostly zipped when Bonita opened the bathroom door.

"What's going on?" she said. She was completely dressed.

"That's my line," Michael replied.

"Why? What's wrong? Who was that on the phone?"

Michael found his shirt and slipped it on without buttoning it. "Where's my gun?" he asked as he rolled up his sleeves.

"It ... it made me nervous just lying there. I moved it over here and put it in the drawer." She pointed to another nightstand on the opposite side of the bed. "I'll get it for you."

"No!" Michael shouted. Hopping as he jabbed his foot into a sock. "Just forget it for now!"

"Michael, what's wrong? Why are you acting like this?"

"I don't know." Michael put on his shoes without lacing them. "Who are you? What's your *real* name?"

"Michael, you know who I am. Why are you acting this way?"

"Yeah? Well, why haven't we been able to find anything on you? The folks in Japan you said you work with don't even know you. They never heard of you."

"It's a mistake! I swear! Check again. I've been there for months."

"Why are you dressed so bright and early this morning? Going somewhere?"

"I ... I couldn't sleep. I didn't want to wake you. I thought I'd go get some breakfast for us somewhere. I was going to have it here when you woke up."

"That's pretty strange behavior for someone who, just a few short hours ago, was afraid to leave the motel, even with police protection. Especially with you being so unfamiliar with the area."

Bonita wiped a tear from her cheek. "I just felt safe. I wanted to surprise you," she said.

Michael forced a brief laugh. "You certainly have all the right answers, don't you?"

Bonita hung her head and stood silent.

"Do you remember when we were in the cemetery after Tiller's funeral?" Michael asked. "You were sleeping in the car. I got worried when you didn't wake up right away. You asked me if I thought someone had gotten your head and hands. Do you remember?"

The blond nodded slowly.

"Bo, I never told you about anyone's hand being cut off."

"Yes you did, Michael!" she blurted. "You told me the day Clevous and the guard were killed at the museum. I ... I got sick, remember?"

"I told you the guard was decapitated. Facts and I never mentioned anything about his hand. Even the news media didn't have that information. The only way you could have known was if you were there. At the time, it just didn't seem important. Maybe I didn't want to think about it because I liked you and you were so sweet and innocent. You had my brain all clouded, but now ... now, I can look back on some of the details and pieces start to fit."

"This is crazy," Bonita said.

"Is it? You were the one that so quickly pointed me toward Sumio Tanaka. I never did feel right about arresting him, but someone kept dumping evidence in my lap. I wonder who that could have been?"

Bonita was silent.

Michael jumped on the bed on his knees and opened the drawer on the nightstand opposite where he had been sleeping. He was surprised to find his gun. "When Facts gets here we're all going to go over to the office for a nice long question and answer session," Michael said, checking his magnum to make sure it was loaded.

"I can't let you do that," Bonita said quietly.

Michael was still on his knees in the center of the bed.

"You don't exactly have any choice, Hon," he said. "I'm going to find out exactly what you know and who you really are."

"I can't let you do that," Bonita repeated. The tears ran down her face.

Michael said, "It's too late to cry now."

"My tears aren't for me." Bonita's voice was cold. "They're for you."

"What are they for ... ?"

Bonita's left foot caught Michael square on his ear, knocking him backwards. He was completely off guard. The force of the kick caused him to drop the heavy magnum on the covers before he went crashing to the floor. Holding the side of his face, Michael scrambled awkwardly to his feet.

"Jeez! You really pack some power," he said as Bonita walked around the bed and approached him.

"You know, it's usually my policy never to hit a lady," he said facing Bo. "I'm going to amend that policy ... starting now." Michael threw a powerful right punch toward Bonita's face. The not-so-defenseless blond delivered a left block that stopped the punch short of its mark. Michael felt as if his arm had been hit by someone swinging a pipe.

After drilling three rapid punches into Michael's mouth, Bonita bent her knees, spun and snatched his arm over her shoulder. Like a rag doll, he flipped over the woman's back and went sailing across the room. Rolls of dust belched from the thin carpet as Michael landed flat on his back. He lay stunned and helpless, withering in pain.

Bonita stepped over the injured detective and went into the bathroom. Michael could hear the shower curtain being moved. Blood dripping from his battered lips and chin, he rolled onto his side and grabbed the arm of an old wooden chair. Using the chair for support, he pulled himself to his feet. His body ached with each breath. Bonita still had her back turned and was doing something in the bathroom. Michael looked at his .357 still sitting in the middle of the covers on the bed. Opportunity was knocking. He took the four steps to the bed and reached for his gun.

Bonita yelled, "Keee-yaa!" and leaped from the bathroom doorway in a perfect flying sidekick across the bed. Just as

Michael's fingertips touched the butt of his magnum, the heel of Bonita's curved foot drilled into the policeman's chest. Once again without his gun, Michael flew backwards, disintegrating the nightstand. The clock and lamp that had been sitting on the flimsy table went to the floor. Although the ceramic base of the lamp was broken and the shade was torn back, the light bulb had survived. Objects in the room cast eerie, long shadows up the walls and ceiling from the unshielded light.

Michael was thankful to discover that being kicked in the chest wasn't nearly as damaging as the flip he had received earlier. Eager to show how unaffected he was by her last blow, Michael quickly stood and faced his attacker. His heart sank. Now he understood what Bonita was doing with the shower curtain. She eased off the bed holding a long samurai sword horizontally across her chest. Her left hand gripped the solid sheath. Her right hand was curled around the braided stainless-steel handle.

"I'm sorry, Michael," she said. "You've brought this on yourself."

"I did? What did I do?" Michael's eyes darted everywhere, looking for anything. To his right was the broken table. Directly in front was Bonita. Unfortunately, she was between him and his magnum on the bed behind her. He looked to the left. Still hanging on the post at the foot of the bed was his hat. Michael was certain he hadn't told Bonita about his hat.

"You have interrupted my father's progress," Bonita said. She moved forward one step.

"Your father?! Who's your father?!" Michael stepped back once.

"Earlier, you asked who I was. It's only fair that you know your executioner," the blond said.

"That's all I want," Michael said nervously looking around. "Just for everything to be fair."

"I am Kascika Tamuri Kudo, daughter of Master Masato Kudo."

"Get outta here. Who are you trying to bullshit? You're not even ..."

"Japanese?" She finished the sentence. "Americans are so ignorant, so quick to stereotype."

"Come on, you've got green eyes and blond hair."

"In the years that followed America's slaughter of thousands of my father's people, he saw the births of one deformed child after another. All victims of the radiation that still haunts my country. He needed a strong healthy child to carry out his dreams. A child from a radiation-free environment. A child that would grow to produce other healthy offspring."

"So, he adopted you."

"Yes, when I was only a few months old. My American mother abandoned me. I was raised and trained in secret by Masato Kudo. He had the money and connections to erase all records of my birth. After cancer claimed my father's wife, he found a greater need for me."

"What was that? What is Kudo up to?"

"I have already talked too much."

"No, Bo, or whatever your name is, don't you see? You've been used, brainwashed. What are you and your father doing?"

"You don't have to be born in Japan," she said, "to be Japanese. I am not brainwashed. I am very Japanese. Educated by a great man who sees the world as it is. My father will never forgive your evil empire for its actions in 1945."

Nineteen forty-five? Michael thought. "Of course, Hiroshima."

"Yes... Hiroshima."

"Did you kill Tiller and the guard that night at the museum?"

"No."

"But, you killed Connie, didn't you?" he asked.

"Her death was more valuable to us than her life at the time."

"And mine?"

"I'm sorry," Kascika said. "Your persistence could interfere with my father's plans. I have no choice."

Michael was well aware of the fate Bo, or more recently Kascika, had in store for him. He snatched up one of the table legs from the broken nightstand and swung at the young samurai. She pulled the sword from its sheath and, in a flash, halved the table leg. Michael moved toward the foot of the bed swinging the remainder of his club in the opposite direction. It was immediately lopped off above his hand. He flung the last bit of the table leg at the woman's face and grabbed his hat from the footboard.

Masato Kudo had trained his daughter well. Her sword flicked twice. The first motion knocked the projectile harmlessly away; the second plucked the hat from Michael's grasp, sending the headpiece rolling atop the bedspread. The hat settled in the center of the bed just inches from the chrome magnum.

Great! Michael thought. The only two weapons he had were lying side-by-side behind a samurai master that wanted him dead. He had to stall. He had to give himself time to think.

"You can't possibly expect to get away with killing a cop." Michael said.

"I will get away with it. When they find you, you will be sliced to bits. I will be gone. They will think the murderer got you and that I am missing."

"Oh come on. Cops aren't as stupid as movies make them out to be. No one will believe that, plus Facts is already on his way. He knows about you!"

"I just have to elude the police for a short while. After that ... it won't matter. If Facts gets here before I leave, there will be a double murder."

"Why won't it matter?" Michael asked. "What's going to happen that it won't matter?"

"I ... I'll be gone. Father owns a private jet. We will be out of the country before any ..."

"You're lying! What's the real reason, Kascika?!"

"No ... I ..."

Michael stepped in quickly. If he were to try her, now would be the time. She was distracted by his harsh accusations. He faked a right punch and threw his left, catching her on the chin. She could take a punch. Kascika didn't even move her feet as she snapped her head around to absorb the force of Michael's left hook.

She immediately countered with an elbow strike to the detective's throat that tumbled him into what would have been a backward somersault had he not hit his head on the heavy wooden chair. Michael rolled on the dirty floor. Both hands clutched the back of his head, reacting to the pain exploding from the rapidly swelling knot. Kascika rubbed her jaw.

"You really pack some power," she said sarcastically. "You know, it's usually my policy not to kill persistent police officers. I'm going to amend that policy ... now." She moved toward Michael.

He rolled to his knees and grabbed the sturdy back of the chair that had nearly cracked his skull. Then, lifting the bottom of the chair at Kascika, he charged, thrusting the four legs into the attack. The green-eyed samurai's sword silently slashed left and right. Whap! Whap! Two chair legs went flying. Michael struck again. Two more legs bounced across the carpet. Michael growled and moved in again with nothing more than the chair back and the thick wooden seat attached to that.

Kascika's blade came down, slicing two-thirds of the way through the seat before becoming stuck in the hard oak fibers. She tugged unsuccessfully to pull the sword from its wooden captor.

With all his strength, Michael threw the chair to the left, the sword swinging with it. Kascika, holding firmly onto the handle, was thrown off balance by the sudden weight shift. Michael dropped, knelt at the foot of the bed, and grabbed a corner of the mattress with both hands.

Kascika shouted, "Keeey-yaa!!!" as she drove her right heel into the chair, shattering the chair and freeing her steel blade.

Michael dug his fingers into the layers of blankets and sheets, then yanked. The covers jumped from the bed toward the policeman; along with them came the hat and chrome magnum. Kascika's reflexes were like lightning. Her sword danced down, then up, scooping the revolver and flinging it across the room into a far corner where it landed with a loud 'thump.'

Michael lay motionless on his back. The covers he had dragged from the bed were now draped over his torso and face.

The female samurai held the sheathed sword in preparation for the next clever trick Michael would try when he sprang from the mountain of sheets. Nothing moved.

"What are you doing?!" Kascika asked in a demanding voice. No answer.

"Damn you, Michael! What are you doing! Come out from under there!"

Still no answer.

She cautiously hooked her foot into the edge of the covers and flipped them away. The charcoal gray dress hat popped loose and rolled in an arc to her feet. Her eyes shifted momentarily to the hat, then back to Michael. He held the derringer steady on his target. No time to waste. No second chances. His fingers squeezed back.

Pap!

The tiny gun rocked slightly. A plume of blue-white smoke curled upward. Kascika clutched at her chest with one hand while the other shook the sheath from the sword. Tears ran down her face.

"No!" she gasped. "I ... will ... not ... fail ... my father!"

She raised the sword above her head and fell to her knees. Michael rotated the barrel of the derringer, locking the second and last live round into place. He again pointed the gun and squeezed the trigger.

Pap!

The samurai woman's sword clattered to the floor as the red stain in her blouse grew darker. She slowly crawled and grabbed Michael's unbuttoned shirt. He started to move away but could detect none of the aggression of the previous attacks. He leaned against the wall and heaved his fallen adversary onto his chest. Kascika tilted her head back, allowing Michael to look into her beautiful green eyes.

"It's over," Michael said pushing the hair out of her face.

"Not for you," she whispered. "I'm sorry."

"Why! What do you mean?"

Her eyes closed. She drew her final breath, and the woman Michael had known as Bonita Baker was dead.

Michael rolled Kascika's body off him and forced his bruised muscles to bring him to a standing position. He looked at the telephone and decided it was too much trouble and picked up his police radio to call for help.

"You sure you don't want an ambulance?" Facts said, handing Michael a fresh cold washcloth to hold against his head.

"Yeah, thanks. Is the lieutenant on the way?"

"The lieutenant, crime lab, a couple district cars, and the coroner."

Michael stood by the curb in front of room fourteen and threw the washcloth on the ground.

"Facts, ol' buddy," Michael said, "I need your help."

"You know you've got it. What's up?"

"We've got to do something now."

"OK, what?"

"We've got to pick up Kudo."

"Yeah, no doubt. It's a good thing you found that bomb. He must be some kind of nut, wantin' to blow up Indy. Imagine, all that money and nothing better to do than try to set off a nuclear bomb and kill a bunch of people."

"I mean, we've got to go ... now!" Michael said.

"Now ... right now?"

Michael nodded and headed back into the motel room.

"Uhhh ... Yo, Michael," Facts said following his partner. "You just can't leave. I mean ... you just shot somebody. You've got to stick around for a report or something. We'll get Kudo. Don't worry about that."

"We don't have time to wait," Michael said. He picked up his derringer from the floor and reloaded it with extra bullets he had hidden in his hat band.

Facts' frustration was beginning to show. "You really shouldn't take that, Michael. You're screwing up the crime scene."

Michael slid the small gun into its pouch and set his hat on his head. He cringed from the initial pain of the hat pressing his tender scalp.

"Why don't you just relax, man?" Facts suggested. "We can rush things along and be done in a couple of hours. Whadda ya say?"

Michael quickly walked around the bed and looked in the corner of the room. He picked up his revolver, examined it for damage and placed it in the leather holster on his belt.

"Ahhhww ... Dude," Facts said. "You can't be doing all this. Moving everything around. Taking your guns. You're gonna get burned good on this, ya know."

Michael looked around the room to make sure he wasn't forgetting anything. "Are you with me?" he asked Facts.

"Leaving the scene of a police-action shooting with a fatality after altering the crime scene. Are you kidding? We'll be suspended for a thousand years for this."

"We'll go fishin'."

"I don't want to go fishin' for a thousand years."

"Are you with me?"

"Why don't we have somebody take a look at that bump on your head?"

"You with me?"

Facts threw his arms up and sighed. "Yes ... I'm with you, damn it," he said.

"Good, you're driving."

Michael turned his reluctant partner and guided him toward the door. On the way out, Facts pointed to Kascika's body lying face up along the front wall of the room.

"What? You're not taking her?" he sarcastically asked. "You've picked up everything else."

Michael gave an extra nudge, forcing the portly policeman out into the early morning air.

As Michael reached to shut the motel room door, he looked at the lifeless body of Kudo's daughter. It was hard to believe this was the same person he had been so enchanted by, he thought. Even in death, even after all that had happened, she still looked so innocent. He had sincerely wanted her to stay when the investigation was over, but now ... Michael looked a moment longer, then eased the door closed. He inhaled and let it out slowly.

"Bo," he whispered under his breath as the latch clicked and locked.

"You all right?" Facts asked.

"Yeah."

"Where are we going, the Omni?"

"Yeah, but first I've got a stop to make. You drive, I'll guide."

Facts pulled out of the parking lot and waved to the uniformed patrolman that was turning into the drive. "Shit! Are we gonna get it now!" he said driving past the confused patrolman to the unknown location Michael so desperately needed to get to.

FOURTEEN

Michael pounded on the heavy door with his fist. "Come on, answer!" he begged.

"Maybe he's in bed," Facts said. "Like everyone else is at this time of morning."

"Well, he's gotta get up."

"Why are we here anyway? Haven't we put this man through enough?"

"Great!" Michael shouted when he heard the latch slide from the other side of the door.

Sumio Tanaka turned on the foyer light to illuminate the faces of the two men that had come calling so early.

"Detective Finder ... Detective Brown, at last you are here."

"What do you mean, at last?" Michael asked.

"I have been expecting you." Sumio bowed. He was dressed in a gray suit with a crisp white shirt and red and gray striped tie. Surprisingly, he already had on his polished black dress shoes. In his left hand was the elegant samurai sword from the shrine in his practice dojo, the same sword that felled his would-be assassins.

"I never thought I would hear myself say this," Michael

said, "but I need your help."

Sumio bowed again. "I am ready."

"How did you know we were coming?" Facts asked.

"I have been meditating. Your being here was inevitable, Mr. Brown," Sumio explained. "I also feel Mizu Kokoro is ready to strike. We must act quickly."

"About Kokoro," Michael said. "The woman you met at the museum, Bonita Baker, is dead. She tried to kill me. I think *she* was your Mizu Kokoro."

Sumio took his hand and gently turned Michael's face toward the light to examine his injuries. "She was your lady friend, wasn't she?" he asked.

"Was," Michael said. "She was really Masato Kudo's daughter. Did you know he had an adopted American daughter?"

"Masato's daughter? No, I didn't know that."

"Yeah, she almost kicked my ass. In fact, my ass was the only thing she didn't kick. She also used a sword like yours. I'm pretty sure she killed Connie ... the woman murdered at the museum."

"If what you say is true," Sumio speculated, "then I do not believe Miss Baker was Mizu Kokoro."

"Why?" Michael asked.

"Two reasons. One ... I am certain that the woman at the museum was not killed by Kokoro. And two ... you fought her this morning."

"So, what's that prove?"

"If she were Kokoro, Michael, you would be dead," Sumio said coldly.

"Well, you don't have to be so blunt about it."

"I'm sorry. Sometimes the truth *is* blunt." Sumio stepped outside, shut the door and locked it.

"Where are we going?" he asked. "We must leave."

"I was hoping you would have the answer to that," Michael said.

"Oh no." Sumio shook his head. "You have been doing just fine in solving the mysteries that have developed. You must find Mizu Kokoro."

"That's all fine and dandy, but what are you going to be doing?"

"I will be close to you because if by chance you do find him, you don't want to be alone."

"Jeez, you guys are givin' me the willies," Facts said looking nervously around Sumio's gardens.

"What do you think about Masato Kudo?" Michael asked. "Could he be Kokoro."

"He kept a daughter for years without my knowledge. Perhaps he has other secrets," Sumio answered.

"What do you think?" Michael turned to his partner.

"Yo, you lost me hours ago. I'm just a driver and a fishing buddy," Facts said.

"Well driver, let's start at the Omni Hotel penthouse and have a talk with Mr. Kudo himself."

The three men climbed into the unmarked police car and headed downtown just as the sunrise was peeking over the Indianapolis skyline.

The air in the lobby of the Omni Hotel was rich with the smell of freshly brewed coffee. Sparkling chandeliers, plush carpet and prim doormen were just examples of the five-star service and accommodations available to any guest who could afford the rooms.

Sumio, Facts and Michael, amid several stares and scowls, boarded one of the mirrored elevators. Facts pushed the button marked "P.H." to start them moving upwards to the seventeenth floor penthouse where Masato Kudo was staying.

"Hold it, please!" a voice called as the elevator doors began to shut.

"Oh no," Michael muttered. He recognized the gravelly voice.

Sumio jabbed the rubber on the doors, causing them to spring open. In walked Major Stan Hamilton. "Good morning, men," he said in a cheery voice. He extended his index finger and poked the "P.H." button to the beat of a tune he was whistling.

"Hello, Major," Facts said dryly. He was actually looking at Michael. Sumio bowed.

"I'm sure this is not the greatest coincidence in the world," Michael said. "What are you doing here, Stan?"

"Oh, nothing." The major stopped whistling long enough to answer. "By the way," he added, "you two are a very hot item. I received a call this morning about a police detective shooting a woman, leaving the body and disappearing. Ohhh ... what your chief wouldn't give to know where you two are right now. I saw him just before I came over here, you know. Whooo-we! I haven't seen a man that mad since I recovered a fumble during a college football game and ran fifty yards in the wrong direction.

Your chief looked a lot like my coach did that day." Stan chuckled to himself, then glanced up to see what floor they were on.

"Is the Chief on his way up also?" Michael asked.

"Naw, I didn't tell him where I was going."

"What made *you* come here?"

"The girl you killed stayed here. She worked for Kudo. He stays here. It stands to reason this is where you were bound to show up."

"She was Kudo's daughter," Michael said.

"Bullshit!"

"No, really. Kudo adopted her. At least that's what she said."

"You believed her?"

"Yeah, why would she lie? She thought she was going to kill me."

"From what I heard about the room at the Inn-D-Inn and from the looks of your face, she had every reason to believe she was going to kill you."

"So are you going to run to the nearest telephone and get us out of your hair once and for all?" Michael asked.

"Hell, no!" Stan said. "I can't turn you two over to the chief now. I need you both alive. I found out from asking around that you guys don't have any notes to hand over to me." Stan looked at Facts. Facts looked at the numbers beside the doors.

"Here's our floor!" he announced.

The elevator doors opened. The four men stepped into a small deserted room located just outside the door to the suite.

"Finder!" Major Hamilton said, turning to face the

detective. "If I try to solve this thing on my own with no more than I have now, I'll be here forever. If I try to throw my weight around to force you to tell, you'll just lie to me. That sets me back even further. I guess the only way I'm going to get home before the snow falls is to let you and Brown do your thing and hope you'll at least let me tag along. Whadda ya say? I'm not totally useless, you know."

"I know," Michael said. His voice had a hint of surrender in it. "Honestly, I think we can use all the help we can get."

The door to the penthouse was ajar.

"It's open," Facts said. Stepping away, he pulled a handkerchief and hastily cleaned his glasses. Michael drew his magnum. Stan and Facts both checked their guns and stood ready. Sumio made no noticeable adjustments.

"Let's go," Michael whispered and moved into the first room of the suite. The three others followed. They found themselves in a lavishly decorated living room. The only light was that of the morning shining through the giant windows on the far wall. Facts and the major went into a room to the left. Michael started down a hallway with Sumio close behind. Halfway to the room at the end of a short corridor, Sumio placed his hand on Michael's arm.

"Someone is here," he whispered.

Michael brought his revolver up to about shoulder level and inched forward. Now he too could hear movement on the other side of the door. He squatted as the door suddenly opened. His finger started to squeeze back. A figure moved in the doorway.

"Eeeeeee!" An old woman screamed. She was dressed in a maid's uniform. The three rolls of toilet paper and box of tissues she was carrying went flying.

"Lord, what do you want?" she cried.

"It's OK," Michael shouted, lowering his gun and holding up his police ID. "We're police officers."

"Well what-a-you tryin' to do, give an old woman a heart attack?"

"Sorry Ma'am. Is Mister Kudo here?"

"No, he left early this morning an' took his crew with him. I thought I'd come up early an' get this ..."

"Where did he go?" Michael interrupted.

"How would I know? All I know is he got outta here earlier today than he ever has. He was in a hurry, too."

"Did he check out?"

"If he did, he didn't take any of his things. His clothes and stuff are still here."

"Can she open this room over here?" Facts asked. He and the major had been watching from the living room. "This door over here is locked."

"Oh, no. I can't let you in there," the maid said. "That's Mr. Kudo's office. We were told not to go in there under any conditions."

"Can you open it?" Michael asked.

"I can, but I'll do nothing of the sort," the maid said defiantly.

"We've got to get in that office!"

"Not without the manager's say so."

"Give me the key, damn it!" Michael reached for the woman.

Sumio quickly intervened, blocking the anxious detective from the stubborn employee.

"I will take care of this," Sumio said. He turned from the maid and Michael, walked swiftly past Stan Hamilton and Facts and across the living room to the locked office door. He thrust forward with a powerful front kick, tearing the heavy door from the door frame and sending it crashing to the side.

"That does it!" the maid shouted, running from the penthouse. "I'm calling security."

Masato Kudo's office, unlike the rest of the tidy suite, was quite cluttered. Reports and folders covered a long walnut desk. Bulletins, charts, and diagrams were on the walls. A computer printer was still rolling out sheet after sheet of data that was stacking on the floor. On the wall above and behind the desk was a huge map of the United States. Japanese characters were printed over the map. The capital of each state was marked with an orange dot.

"Looks like Kudo was running all of Ku-Tech Enterprises from here," Michael said, scanning over some files.

"Yo, Michael, look at this." Facts was standing in front of a tack board. He carefully removed a tack and pulled a photograph from the collection of photos and letters pinned to the cork.

Michael stepped next to Facts and looked at the picture he held. It was a black and white photo of Masato Kudo, a slightly younger Japanese woman, and a pre-teenage American girl with a sweet little smile.

"That must be Bo," Michael said.

"And Masato's wife," Sumio added from over Facts' other shoulder. He studied some of the other photos on the board. For the first time since they had left the fragrant gardens of his home, Sumio set his sword down. He reached with both hands and pulled a cracked and yellowed photo of a Japanese woman and man. They were in their thirties, smiling and holding hands.

"Who are they?" Facts asked.

"My father and mother," Sumio answered softly. "I had believed all photos of them had been lost."

"You mean you never had any pictures of your family?"

"Oh, I have an unlimited number of photographs of all of my family and friends ... in my heart."

After a long look, Sumio tacked the photo back on the board.

"They never wear out." He picked up his sword. "They are never lost." He turned to look out across the city from the seventeenth floor view. "And they are in brilliant color," he said.

"I've seen this garbage before," Major Hamilton muttered from across the office. He was reading the computer printouts from the floor behind the printer. "I have no idea what this stuff is, but I've seen it at Stockford. It's coded somehow."

"Could the information on that stolen disk be used here?" Michael asked.

"No, that was just some useless bullshit. This is different, somehow." Major Hamilton put his gun away. "I don't get it," he said. "Why would he want to blow up Indianapolis?"

Michael snapped his magnum back into his holster.

"Well, it's centrally located," he said looking at the map on the wall behind the desk. He tipped his hat back and shoved his hands into his pockets.

Facts was looking at some statistics on Ku-Tech Enterprises that he had found on the desk. Sumio stared out the window. Stan Hamilton read the printouts rolling from the computer. The room grew quiet, but each man's mind reeled with possibilities.

"Hey! Wait a minute!" Michael said, breaking the silence. "Chicago's not a state capitol ... and there're two dots in California. What is this?"

Stan joined Michael beneath the map. "Yeah, there're spots over Dallas and Houston."

"I know," Facts said. "Those are the cities where his art show toured. I saw the list."

"That would make sense," Michael said. "But there's a little 'X' on Indy's orange dot. Why would they scratch off that one? They completed their show here and Kudo didn't succeed in blowing up the city. So why are we marked out?" He looked at Facts, then Stan.

"I don't know ..." Major Hamilton said, "... but that green dot there," he pointed to a spot just under Indianapolis, "is about where Stockford is. I know it's not printed anywhere, but that's about where it's physically located."

Hands in his pockets, hat still tipped back, Michael began to pace. "What have we got here?" he wondered out loud.

"Yo, let's take a look at the whole deal," Facts said. "Masato Kudo gets pissed off at the United States over Hiroshima. He's also a little pissed at Mr. Tanaka over some personal bullshit or something. So then he acts like he's sharing his rare art collection with Indy, while in reality he's setting up a nuclear bomb. Sort of Kudo's version of 'two birds with one stone,' I guess. Then you, Michael, find his little bomb and ruin his plans. Well, we already know Kudo is a vengeful fucker. He then sends his secret weapon daughter after Michael. Michael finds out what's happening and kills Kascika. We show up here to put the clamps on Kudo and, of course, he's gone."

"That wouldn't be too big of a problem," Major Hamilton said. "We could scramble a couple of fighters to intercept his jet. If he refuses to turn back, he would be blown out of the sky."

Sumio turned from the window. He and Michael looked at each other.

"There's more to it than that, isn't there?" Michael asked.

Sumio looked out the window again. "I don't know," he said. "You are the detective. I am just Sumio Tanaka."

Michael looked up at the map. "Why the 'X'?" he said. "What don't we have that all those other cities *do* have?"

"We had the art show," Facts said.

"Yeah."

"He didn't blow up the city," Stan added.

"Yeah," Michael agreed again. After a pause he said, "Oh my God!"

"What?!" Major Hamilton and Facts asked in unison.

"I know what we don't have. We don't have that bomb anymore. What if Kudo left a nuclear bomb in every city on his tour? Cookie said that bomb I found was set up to be detonated by a remote signal. He said that no one could set it off without blowin' themselves up, but what if they could? What if the signal came from far enough away that you could blow up a city, or several cities, from far away?"

"From his jet!" Facts shouted.

"No," Major Hamilton said, "A satellite!" He spun and pointed at the computer printer. "That's where I saw a code like that, at Stockford, in their control room after the murders."

"What exactly do they do at Stockford?" Michael asked Stan. "Can they send a signal to a satellite from there?"

"Why, yes. They send and receive messages all the time. But it's all closed down. There's no one working there now. Just a couple of guards."

"All that much easier for someone to use it," Michael said. "Don't you see?! He used the same stunt at Stockford that he used here at the art museum. He staged a robbery where a computer disk was taken to cover the fact he was actually leaving something inside. You said yourself that the disk was useless."

Major Hamilton nodded slowly. "Yeah," he said.

"Look." Michael continued. "Ku-Tech Enterprises has the technology to come up with some kind of transmitter. Don't they have satellites?"

Facts thought for a moment. "Yo!" he said. "They have two. Hoshi, launched February 2nd, 1987. And another one, Chitchai Kodomo, on September 6th, 1988. Both are listed as communication satellites."

"Facts, you're great!" Michael said. "You see, a signal transmitted from Stockford to one or both of those satellites could simultaneously detonate the bombs hidden all over the country. He's already planted the transmitter somewhere in Stockford, so I imagine it's on some kind of timer."

"A simultaneous detonation of nuclear bombs in every major city in the United States would be devastating," Stan said.

"We've got to contact the authorities in each city."

"When would he have the timer set?"

"Today," Sumio said still looking out across the city.

"Why today?" Michael asked.

"Today is August 6th."

Michael thought for a second then said, "Hiroshima!"

"This is the anniversary," Sumio said. "I remember all too well." He left the window and approached the other men. "This is when he would do his deed and this is the type of deed Mizu Kokoro would be involved in," he said.

"Facts, what can you tell me about the bombing of Hiroshima?" Michael asked.

"Well, let's see. The bomb was dropped by a B-29 bomber, named the Enola Gay. The crew nicknamed the bomb 'Little Boy.' Like Mr. Tanaka said, it was in 1945, August 6th, at 8:15 in the morning. Over one hundred thousand people killed, but other estimates claim ..."

"Eight fifteen!" Michael shouted.

Stan looked at his watch. "It's ten after 6:00," he said.

"If that's when all of this is going to take place, we don't have time to call every city," Michael said. "We certainly don't have time to go searching around Stockford. I think our best chance is to stop Kudo. He's probably on his way to the airport, trying to get the hell out of the country while he can."

"If he's not gone already," Facts said.

"That's a chance we'll have to take. If we can keep him on the ground, he may tell us how to shut down the transmitter. If he was suicidal, he wouldn't have used a timer in the first place."

"Who's to say he did use a timer? How do we know if he's even trying to get to the airport?" Major Hamilton was being the pessimist.

"Any better ideas?" Michael asked.

The four men hurried to the elevator. As they rode down to the lobby, Sumio looked at Michael. "Did you notice the name of the second satellite?" he asked the detective.

"What about it?"

"It roughly translates to mean, a small boy or 'little boy.'"

"Oh, jeez," Facts said.

The elevator doors opened and the race to the airport began.

FIFTEEN

Indianapolis International Airport was busy, even at 6:32 in the morning. Facts, Michael, Major Hamilton and Sumio left their cars in the middle of the lower-level drive and ran into the terminal. They were greeted by a middle-aged airport police officer as soon as they passed through the second set of automatic doors.

"Did you get our message?" Michael asked the policeman.

"Yeah, no big deal. We've got everything under control. Why in the world didn't ... "

"No time for that!" Michael interrupted. "What did you find out?"

"Relax, man. We've only got two flights leaving this morning that have flight plans that will take them anywhere near Japan. Flight 333 at gate seventeen east doesn't leave for another couple of hours and a private jet owned by some big wheel that was due to leave now. We called the tower and they've canceled the departure clearance until you guys figure out if this is the one you want."

"That sounds like it. Where is it now?"

"Out on the airfield waiting for clearance."

"Let's get going," Michael said, urging the airport officer

to lead the way. He led them through a series of hallways and stairwells until their small group burst out onto the paved acreage of the airfield.

"That's the one!" The airport officer pointed to a sleek medium-sized black jet rolling away from the terminal. "Hey, where's he going?!"

Another uniformed guard ran up. "Dispatch just called!" he said, almost frantic. "That jet's ignoring the tower's orders to cancel departure clearance. And they're not answering their radio."

"Shit! Do you guys have a car handy?" Michael asked.

"Not handy. It's in the parking garage."

Michael looked underneath the tail section of a huge 727 jetliner that was refueling. Across from the refueling area was the emergency medical depot. Several long bright yellow fire trucks and a few smaller yellow ambulances were parked out front.

"Come on!" Michael motioned toward the depot. "We've got to stop him!" He ran for the medical building with the others in close pursuit.

Michael climbed into the driver's seat of a big ladder truck sitting fueled and ready. He turned the key and the monstrous engine rumbled. The passenger door opened and Sumio pulled himself up into the seat next to Michael.

"No, Sumio, you'd better stay here," Michael warned. "This isn't going to be a sightseeing tour."

"You must not be alone with Masato. I will go where you go." Sumio pointed to the black jet making its way down the taxi lane. "And you must go now!" he said.

Michael pulled away, barreling across the airfield after

Masato's jet. The aircraft turned onto the runway, paused briefly, and began to increase the thrust from its powerful engines.

"I can't get to him in time," Michael said, "but I can get to about the middle of that runway." He drove across a grassy patch, exploding a taxi light with the front bumper of the fire truck. The whine of the jet's engines turned into a roar as the craft moved down the runway, increasing its speed by the second. After obliterating a series of taxi and landing lights, the yellow fire truck bounced onto the runway in the path of the departing jet and stopped.

"Let's hope he wants to live," Michael said, gritting his teeth.

Sumio sat calmly. They both watched the nose of the jet dip as the pilot aborted the take-off attempt and desperately began braking.

Forty yards ... thirty ... then twenty. The black jet still had too much momentum.

"He's not going to be able to stop!" Michael said squeezing the large steering wheel and closing his eyes. Within fifty feet the aircraft veered sharply to the right. Its left wing skimmed just inches above the fire truck.

Michael opened his eyes and looked down to the end of the vacant runway. "What happened?" he asked. "Where'd it go?"

"There." Sumio pointed with the hilt of his sword out the passenger window. "They are going to try another runway," he said.

Masato's jet turned onto the end of a different runway that ran at about a forty-five degree angle from the other. Michael reeled the truck into the tightest U-turn possible and headed for the alternative strip. The jet's engines again roared, starting the plane on another take-off. Michael drove onto the runway well ahead of the jet, and steered straight for the aircraft. Long before the two vehicles came as dangerously close as they had before, Masato's jet turned sharply, spinning the craft completely around and off the paved surface. Instantly the rugged jet rolled across the grass patch of airfield and up onto the taxi lane.

"Oh shit!" Michael exclaimed. "They're going to use the taxi way. That's a straight shot from here!"

The jet was directly in front of the fire truck and moving away. Michael pressed the gas pedal to the floorboard but was no match for the plane's powerful engines. The gap between the two widened, as the pilot opened up full throttle in anticipation of his hard-earned lift-off. Michael's hopes of intervening with the fleeing Masato were lost.

"Damn it!" Michael shouted. He eased off the gas pedal, realizing the uselessness of the pursuit. Then, out of the corner of his eye, he saw it. Another bright yellow fire truck, flashing lights, siren blaring, charging perpendicular to the taxi way.

Facts leaned out of the passenger window and gave a thumbs-up sign as Major Hamilton boldly rushed into the path of the escaping aircraft.

There was a reduction in power and the front of the plane dropped steeply as its pilot desperately tried to avoid a collision with the second fire truck. The jet went out of control, skidding into a violent fishtail. The right tire burst, driving the disabled craft from the pavement.

"All right!" Michael cheered. He drove the fire engine along the left side of Masato's jet. The other truck, with Major Hamilton at the wheel, closed in on the right side. Flanked by the two fire trucks, the grounded black jet limped toward the terminal.

"We've got him!" Michael said smiling. He looked over at the solemn Sumio. "Well, come on, man, cheer up. I realize we're not out of hot water yet, but we have him."

"You have nothing," Sumio said. "You have cornered a very dangerous, desperate man in a crowded airport. Do not celebrate prematurely ... and Michael ..." Sumio placed his hand on the detective's arm. "... Don't underestimate what we have here or all will be lost."

Michael could not remember ever seeing a more serious face than the one he was looking into at that moment. Sumio's mood drained the excitement from his soul.

"What the hell is he doing?" Michael asked when his attention turned back to the jet. It was rolling toward a part of the terminal where the new restaurant had been opened just weeks before. The restaurant was an oasis in the otherwise hectic boarding area. The three stories of broad tinted windows delivered an impressive view of the airfield to its dining guests.

"What the hell is going on?!" Michael shouted. "He's not going to stop."

The patrons in the restaurant could also sense that something wasn't quite right with the sinister black aircraft slowly rolling in their direction. At first only a few looked from their breakfast plates or morning papers. Then, as the plane came closer, more and more took notice.

Michael accelerated from behind the wing to see if he could get the pilot's attention. As the fire truck pulled alongside the cockpit, Michael could see the pilot slumped over the controls. His blood ran down the inside of the windshield. Payment for his failure to escape.

The movement in the restaurant increased. Some moved from their tables. A chair fell. A waitress dropped her tray. There was a scream. Another chair and table went down. There were more screams as the wave of panic swept over the crowded room. Parents grabbed their children, commuters abandoned their briefcases. Total havoc erupted as everyone stampeded for the exits.

The nose of the pilotless jet met the windows of the restaurant with a deafening crash. The unfortunate few that were still inside were pelted by chunks of plaster and flying slivers of jagged glass. The jet penetrated the building as far as its wings, then stopped. Billows of smoke and dust curled from the damaged restaurant. Arms and legs protruded from the rubble, some moving, some not. People wandered injured and confused, calling for lost companions. The door to the plane, located just in front of the wing, opened. Major Hamilton and Facts were running from under the tail section of the jet, weapons drawn. Michael and Sumio were also on foot.

Masato Kudo appeared in the open doorway. He was dressed in the traditional black gown of his ancient samurai style. A band ran across his forehead and through his gray hair. A sword hung from his side.

"Masato!" Sumio called out to his childhood friend. "End this madness, Masato. Enough have suffered. We have discovered your evil plan."

Kudo leaped from the door of the plane and disappeared in the smoke of the restaurant's ruins.

"Kudo, stop!" Michael shouted. The four men ran into the chaotic terminal to look for the killer. They were struggling against the flow of rescue workers and curiosity seekers en route to the scene of the crash. Michael, Facts, Sumio and Major Hamilton ended up in front of the airport terminal. Two cab drivers were arguing and pointing.

"Have you seen a guy in a black outfit with glasses and a sword on his side?" Michael asked the drivers.

"The son-of-a-bitch just took off in my cab!" the smaller of the two drivers said.

"Which way?"

"How the fuck do I know?" the angry driver answered.

Michael looked at the larger one.

"We need your cab," he said.

"Fuck you, asshole!" the barrel-chested cabby growled. He snatched the stub of a chewed cigar from his mouth and threw it on the ground. "You ain't takin' shit!"

Sumio stepped around Michael. He grabbed the driver by the ear and hurled him over a barricade.

"Let's go," Sumio said, and climbed into the back seat.

Michael jumped into the driver's seat. Facts sat beside him. Stan was next to Sumio.

"I think he's headed for Stockford," Michael said as he drove out of the arrivals area.

Major Hamilton said, "I agree."

"How long will it take us from here?"

"About twenty minutes, maybe more."

Facts looked at his watch. 7:40.

Michael accelerated.

The gates at Stockford Army Station were open. They were twisted and bent. The stolen taxicab was parked several feet inside, driver's door open, motor running. Beside the left rear wheel a guard's headless body was sprawled. Not far away, a second guard lay dead, blood oozing from a hole in his chest. Michael slid to a stop and threw the car into park.

Major Hamilton got out and knelt beside one of the slain guards. He then looked across to "A" Building where the giant satellite pointed upward. The outer doors to the building had been shattered.

"I'm gonna kill this little bastard myself!" he screamed. Outraged, the army officer drew his gun and charged the entrance of the building.

"No, Stan!" Michael ran after the major. "No!" he shouted again as he ran up behind the angered man and tackled him. Facts dove on top of the struggling pair to help contain the major.

"Let me go, damn you, Finder!" Major Hamilton pleaded.

"No, Stan, listen to me," Michael said.

"Listen to him!" Facts added. "He knows what he's doing!"

Michael spoke again. "This is no ordinary man. Look at what he's done to heavily armed soldiers with just a sword."

"He knows what he's saying," Facts said. "It would be suicide."

"I need you out here," Michael said. "I've got a plan. Sumio and I must go in. At least with Sumio we have a better chance."

"He's right!" Facts agreed. "Think, man, we don't have much time. Michael and I have been partners a long time. He knows what he's doing."

The major took a deep breath. "What do you need me to do?" he asked.

"You know your way around," Michael explained. "I need you to cut the power to the building as we go in."

Facts said, "Yeah, listen to him, he ... What? Cut the power? Are you crazy? This guy kills heavily armed people in well-lit rooms, and you want to go in there with just your magnum and Sumio's sword in the dark. You're nuts! Don't listen to him, Stan."

"No! I've been thinking about this," Michael said. "If this transmitter thing runs off the power of the building, then when the power's cut, we disarm it."

"So why go in the building at all?" Stan asked. ""Why not just cut the power and wait for Kudo to come out?"

"I don't think Kudo's that stupid. If I've thought of that, then so has he. Facts said that Ku-Tech Enterprises' stock went up because of some kind of super battery. They were working on a battery that could produce extremely high voltage for an extended period of time."

"If it's hooked up to something like that," the major asked, "then what difference will it make to cut the power?"

"Maybe none, but if it's on a battery and the power to the building is off, then anything in there that still makes noise or has any lights on it will probably be the transmitter. It could help me find it. Then if Sumio can keep Kudo away from me long enough, I just might be able to shut the thing down."

Facts looked at his watch. "We've only got thirteen minutes."

"OK, let's get going." Michael looked at his partner. "Facts, I need you to stay with the Major."

"No way, man! If you're crazy enough to go in there, then I'm sure going with you."

"No, listen. You've read all of the stats on Ku-Tech's satellites. You're a walking manual on them. As soon as Stan cuts the power, get on the phone and use his pull to contact one of the other Army bases like this one. With the knowledge you have, Facts, maybe they can figure out where the satellite is and blow it out of the sky."

"Why will we need to do that if you're going to take care of it down here?" Facts asked.

"It's in case we don't make it."

"I still don't think we'll have time," the major said.

"Just try," Michael answered. He looked down beside one of the guards' bodies. "Here," he said picking up a walkie-talkie. "Get the other one of these from the other guard. Our police radios won't work this far from the city but these will. I'll try to stay in contact."

"Yo, Michael!" Facts called. He reached inside his suit jacket and unholstered his .38. "Here," he said throwing the gun. "You never know, and don't scratch it up."

Michael nodded and tucked it in the back of his waistband. He motioned for Sumio, and the two entered "A" Building. Major Hamilton and Facts headed for the main power boxes.

"He will be like a mother bird defending her nest," Sumio said as he and Michael began walking the lit corridor. Sumio held his samurai sword horizontally, one hand on the hilt, the other on the sheath. Michael held his magnum in his right hand and the walkie-talkie in his left.

"Shouldn't you have that thing out of the sheath?" he asked.

"I will handle the sword. You concentrate on the transmitter ... and put that gun away. It will be useless in here."

"Just the same, I'm gonna keep it out."

There was a click. The entire building went completely dark.

"Here we go!" Michael said. He groped around trying to get some sense of direction. "I can't see shit in here. I thought Stan said they had backup lights."

The coal black hall was deathly quiet.

"Sumio?"

"I am here. Be quiet."

There was another click and the battery-powered emergency lights kicked on, forming islands of light in a sea of darkness.

"All right," Michael said. "There's a large maintenance room at the end of this hall. Stan said the base of the transmitting dish was in a fenced-in area inside that room. That's where I think we need to go."

"Be quiet."

"Do you hear something?"

"Shhhhh!"

Sumio tensed and snatched his sword from the sheath.

Clang!

Clang!

Ping!

He struck three times into the blackness, hitting an invisible blade each time. His blade returned to the sheath.

"Jesus!" Michael shouted. "Was that him? I didn't see a thing."

A dark figure popped up, black against the next patch of light.

"There!" Michael pointed his gun and squeezed the trigger.

Ka-blam!!

Again Sumio's sword struck steel.

Clang! Shhhing!

"What?"

"Michael, put ... the gun ... away!"

"Sumio, I almost got him!"

"You almost got *me*. Put the gun away."

Michael reluctantly returned his revolver to his holster.

"How's it going in there?" Facts' voice came over the walkie-talkie.

"Oh, we're having a blast," Michael said. "How are things out there?"

"Slow. Stan's on the phone now. It doesn't look hopeful on our end."

"Keep trying," Michael said. "We're coming up on the room now."

"Eight minutes," Facts warned before setting his radio down.

The room that housed the hydraulics and maintenance

equipment for the workings of the satellite dish was much larger than Michael expected. Two emergency spotlights illuminated a wide area just inside the double doors. Further in the back of the room were the complex mechanisms of the dish's base, blocked off with a wall of chain link fencing. Signs mounted on the fence warned of high voltage and restricted access to authorized personnel only. The single gate stood ajar. There was another emergency light inside this area directed toward worktables and boxes of tools.

"Here it is," Michael said pushing the gate open. He studied the conglomeration of wires, meters and gauges that fed the massive unit. Sumio stood in the light facing the outer doors.

After removing several panels, Michael noticed two olive green wooden boxes sitting to the side. Although the boxes blended well with the surrounding government property, they stood out. Grabbing a large screwdriver from one of the tool boxes, Michael began to pry on the front instead of the top of the first box, a practice he had decided on since the discovery of the bomb in the museum.

"Bingo!" he shouted when the flashing lights of the portable mini-transmitter flickered in his face.

There was a digital timer wired into the system. The white numerals were counting down the time. Five minutes, fifty-seven seconds, ... fifty-six ... fifty-five. Michael tried to turn a knob that should have stopped the timer, but it was locked in the 'on' position. He started to rip some wires loose but thought better of it. If this super battery was as powerful as he had heard, that might not be a good idea. A cable ran from this box to the next. Michael quickly pried the front off that one.

"Shit!" he said.

There were not one, but three thick bundles of dynamite, all linked into the network of wires and switches.

"I wouldn't advise disturbing my little set-up too much, Mr. Finder." Masato Kudo's voice came from the other side of the fence. He was inside the larger room. Both hands gripped the handle of his sword as it rested in the sheath on his side.

Sumio stood facing him, slightly crouched, his sword horizontal. He was silent, focusing all of his attention on the dangerous swordsman.

Michael glanced at the timer. Five minutes, three seconds were left.

"You see, Mr. Finder," Masato continued, "if you try to stop the timer without disarming the explosives, you will ... well... Let's just say, you will cause considerable damage."

"What's to keep me from stuffing my foot in this box and blowing the building sky high and all of us along with it?" Michael said pulling his magnum from under his jacket.

"You are a survivor, Mr. Finder. I know your type. As long as there is time on that clock you will try to stay alive and win the game. The only difference is that in this game, by the time you realize you have lost, it will be too late."

Michael moved out of the cage-type room, pointed his revolver at Masato, and fired. The shot missed. Masato tumbled into a somersault, coming up on his feet between Sumio and Michael.

"You fool," he laughed. "You cannot stop me." He turned to the silent Sumio. "And what a fool you are. You were always so predictable. That's what made you so easy to use. I knew you would be here to try to save your friends. You never had any surprises. You are just an old fool that has forgotten his heritage!"

Sumio's blade lashed out as did Masato's. The sound of their swords colliding echoed in the underground room. Sumio struck down hard. Masato's sword blocked up then slashed down through the front of Sumio's suit jacket, spinning him. Michael aimed, resting his sights directly on Masato's chest. He fired and once again missed.

Sumio slashed at his opponent like lightning. First left, then right, then left again. Masato spun. His sword moved invisibly to an untrained eye. Sumio stepped back. A spot under his right shoulder was red with blood. His stony expression gave no indication of pain.

"Is everything OK in there?" Facts' voice came over the walkie-talkie.

Michael fired again with no results. Sumio stepped in. Masato's sword flicked, knocking the point of Sumio's sword away. He thrust forward. Sumio gasped as the cold steel entered his body. Masato yanked his blade back, ripping flesh and muscle. Sumio Tanaka stumbled back, dropped to his knees, gave one last sorrowful look at Michael, then fell face down in his own blood.

Michael felt a burning feeling in the pit of his stomach as he realized he was suddenly alone with Mizu Kokoro. He could see the timer through the fence. Three minutes, fifty seconds and counting.

"Michael, answer me. Is everything all right in there?" Facts asked.

"No!" the detective answered into the walkie-talkie, then tossed the radio to the floor.

Masato bounced, slid, and rolled toward the lone policeman.

Michael fired twice more.

Ka-blam!

Ka-blam!

Masato did a flip and landed on his feet in front of the detective.

"I believe that's six shots for you, Mr. Finder," he said. "Why don't you drop your weapon."

Michael pointed the gun towards Masato's chest and pulled the trigger.

Click.

"Just checking," he said and dropped the gun off to the side.

"I have heard a little of the news this morning," Masato said. "I understand you have killed my daughter ... with a second weapon. Remove it!" The anger was easy to detect in his voice. "If you have the urge to test my speed, please feel free."

Michael's hand started for his hat, then stopped at his shoulder to brush off some imaginary dust. He then reached into the back of his waistband and slowly pulled Facts' .38.

"Throw it!" Masato ordered.

Michael threw the revolver into the dark.

"Now we will wait for the end of the United States of America!" the vengeful man said. "Then I will cut off your head."

"Well, that's pretty interesting," Michael said, cautiously removing his hat. He turned to look at the timer again. Three minutes. Michael used the hat to hide the derringer slipping into his hand.

Masato could sense something about to happen. He looked into the policeman's poker face then down at the dress hat. Without warning the sword flashed. Michael felt a sharp pain from his right hand. His hat, practically sliced in half, disappeared behind a work bench. The derringer clattered across the floor. Masato cried out and froze. His sword did not return to the sheath as always before, but merely hung by the warrior's side.

Michael held up his hand. His right index finger was gone. Blood poured from the stump where the finger had been, splattering in a puddle at his feet.

"Oh God!" Michael gasped. He clasped his trembling hands together. He felt as though he would vomit. "Don't panic," he kept saying to himself. "Don't panic!" The blood continued to flow, dripping between his fingers.

Michael sucked in a deep breath attempting to control himself. His adrenaline was rushing. A pulse pounded in his throat. *What's he waiting for?* Michael thought. *Why doesn't he finish me off?*

Ignoring his victim for some reason, Masato was slowly, painfully turning. As Kudo's body rotated, Michael could see the reason for the samurai's distraction. Protruding from his back was the gleaming, crafted sword of Master Sumio Tanaka buried between Masato's shoulder blades. Michael, and now Masato, looked to where Sumio was lying. He had propped himself up on one elbow. His right arm was returning to his side, after the precision throw of his magnificent sword.

Sumio smiled at Masato. "Surprise," he said weakly before his head dropped.

Masato stumbled, then fell heavily face down onto the cement floor. Michael started for Sumio, thought for a moment, then checked the timer. It showed one minute, fifty-eight seconds. He was physically and emotionally drained. Pain radiated up his right arm. He picked up the walkie-talkie and staggered back into the caged room with the bomb and the transmitter.

"Facts?" he said into the radio. "You there?"

"Yo, Michael, what's wrong?"

"Are they gonna be able to destroy the satellite?"

"Not in time. It's not like ordering a pizza."

"How close to the building are you?"

"We're right outside. Why?"

"I want you and Stan to move as far away as you can."

"What for?"

"We don't have time for this man, just do it, will you?"

"What are you going to do, Michael?"

"Just do it!" Michael stepped back to get ready to kick the timer and detonate the dynamite.

"Whatever you're planning," Facts said, "think of something else. I'm not budging."

"Have it your way, buddy," Michael said without pushing the transmit button on the walkie-talkie. He swung his leg back then brought it forward to stomp the wires in front of him. "I sure wish Cookie was here," he muttered. As Michael's foot swung, he suddenly stopped himself, hopping to absorb the momentum. "Cookie!!" he said out loud, "Of course. Facts!" he said into the radio.

"You son-of-a-bitch." Facts' complaint blared through the

speaker. "You locked the inside doors behind you. We can't get in!"

"Don't worry about that now," Michael said. "When Cookie defused the bomb at the museum he said it was a hard one to figure out, but easy once you knew how."

"Yeah ... yeah right."

"Facts, he wrote his notes and you read them. We have the steps, we just have to do them."

"Yeah! ... Yeah!" Facts replied. "I'm thinking."

Michael returned to the toolbox and found a pair of wire cutters.

"OK, Michael, listen." Facts' voice came over the walkie-talkie.

"Go ahead!" Michael said, kneeling in front of the dynamite. The timer clicked to fifty-nine seconds.

"Michael, look for a bunch of wires all taped together. They're all different colors," Facts began.

"I see 'em!" Michael said. "Just keep talking." He set the radio down.

"Cut the red and white wire and the green wire."

Michael was struggling in the dim light and with the pain and blood from his finger.

"Now, Michael," Facts continued, "strip the insulation from the end of the green wire that is closest to the power source."

Michael visually traced the wire to the super battery, then followed his instructions. The next several steps were simple and Michael performed them with as little difficulty as possible. The field of focus narrowed to a red wire and a black wire.

Then Facts said, "OK, you have to clip one of those two wires. The wrong one and it's all over."

Michael had the two wires in question bent away from the rest so he could get to the key one quickly. He reached down and picked up the radio. "So which one is it?" he said holding the wire cutter ready.

"Uh ... Oh Jeez no! ... Uh ... uh, I can't remember. I can't think, damn it!!"

"Just relax, man," Michael said. "Just take it easy and think."

The timer read twenty-eight seconds.

"Shit, Michael. I can't think!!"

"Never mind," Michael said, "I just clipped one."

"You did?"

"Yeah, we were out of time and I had to take a chance. Nothing blew up, so I guess that was the right one." Michael faked a laugh. There were eighteen seconds.

"Whew!" Facts said. "That was close. I'm sorry, man."

"No problem," Michael said. He took a deep breath to sound as relaxed as possible. "Uh ... Facts ... Now that the pressure's off, just out of curiosity, which one was it? It's so dark in here I can't even tell what color the wire is I cut." He glanced at the timer. Eleven seconds left.

"It's funny how that affects me," Facts laughed. "Now, let's see ..."

The timer ticked to four seconds.

"It was the red one," he said.

Michael slipped the cutters over the red wire and clipped it in half. He reached into the next box and ripped loose a handful of wires. The timer froze on one second, then went blank. If Michael didn't feel so bad, he probably would have laughed.

"Everything *is* OK, isn't it?" Facts asked.

"Yeah," Michael said. "Everything's fine. I'll be out in a few minutes. We're gonna need an ambulance or something. Can you help me with that?"

"Sure, who's hurt?"

"Well, Sumio's hurt pretty bad and I could use a little attention."

"We'll get someone started."

Michael put the walkie-talkie down. He sat on his knees in front of the disabled battery-powered transmitter. He again clutched the stub where his finger had been. The pain was ten times worse now. He began to stand. The sound of labored breathing through a mixture of blood and mucous came from over Michael's shoulder. He spun.

Masato Kudo loomed precariously above, pointing his sword down with both hands. Masato lunged at the kneeling policeman. Michael dodged to one side. The blade of the sword narrowly missed the detective's neck and jammed deep into the twisted mass of wires and cables surrounding the ultra powerful battery.

There was a loud pop followed by a ball of sparks launching toward the ceiling as Masato's sword sliced through protective insulation, bringing strong positive and negative currents together. Bright blue and white arcs of electricity raced up the steel sword, bonding the samurai's hands to the hilt. Masato's body violently spasmed as thousands of battery-generated volts entered like tiny lightning strikes. Sparks popped and shot around the room. Flames leaped from control panels. Melting wires and insulation began to blacken the air with their smoke. A scream escaped Masato's throat, distorted by his uncontrollable shaking. His hair smoked. A shower of sparks and fire ignited his cotton garb. The smell of burning flesh increased as the evil samurai was engulfed in flames.

Michael scurried along the floor trying to avoid the glaring red sparks that were spraying throughout the chamber. The electrical claw that had snagged Masato finally released its grip. His burning body fell across the box containing the three bundles of dynamite. Almost immediately the dry pine began to catch fire.

Michael crawled over to Sumio. The air was quickly becoming harder to breathe. "We've got to get out of here!" Michael said. "That dynamite's gonna blow!"

"I cannot walk," Sumio said. "Leave me."

"Leave you, my ass," Michael said. After grabbing and pulling and rolling, he at last managed to heave the wounded man onto his shoulder. He turned and looked through the chain link wall. Pieces of burning wood were already falling directly onto the sizzling explosives. Michael carried Sumio through the doors and, as best he could, trotted toward the exit. Stan and Facts caught Sumio as soon as Michael burst into the fresh air.

"I don't know how big of an explosion that stuff will make," Michael coughed, "but we're getting ready to find out." Lifting the Fushigi Sh'Kata instructor, the three men ran from "A" Building, seeking shelter behind the nearest taxicab.

Ka-woooommm!!!!

The ground rumbled. The windows of the other buildings shattered. A white ball of fire roared hundreds of feet into the air, devouring the satellite dish from underneath.

A massive crater now occupied the place where "A" Building had been. Chunks of smoldering debris began to fall back to earth. Major Hamilton inspected his injuries.

"How's it look?" Michael asked.

"Not real good," Stan said. "We need to get him to a hospital."

"Michael, your hand!" Facts noticed the caked blood covering his clutched fingers. "What happened?"

"Masato wasn't real pleased with me. He got my finger. I suppose it could have been a lot worse."

"Yeah. It could have been *my* finger!"

The rotors of the rescue helicopter could be heard in the distance, chopping the morning sky. Further off in the countryside, the wail of sirens was approaching.

Facts took a white handkerchief from his pocket and pressed it gently against the stump of Michael's index finger. "You still going to be able to hold a fishing pole?" he asked.

"I'm sure gonna find out."

Facts put his arm around Michael's shoulder as they crouched behind the car.

"Where's my gun?" he asked.

"Get outta here."

Share the Excitement
Order books for your friends

Art of Vengeance   _____
by Mel J. McNairy   # copies x $10.95
An Indianapolis police detective tries to unravel the horrifying secrets surrounding gruesome murders.
$10.95 each

Also available from Filibuster Press:

The Break Room   _____
by Kyle Hannon   # copies x $10.95
A talented builder finds profit in the inner city, but he must first triumph over urban politics and media harassment.
$10.95 each

With A Smile Upon His Face   _____
by Mike Delaney   # copies x $10.95
Follow one man's inspiring journey from an Indiana farm to the top of the world.
$10.95 each

sub total	_____
IN residents add 5% sales tax	_____
Shipping: $1.95 for first book	
and 75¢ for each additional	_____
TOTAL	_____

SHIP TO:

Name: _____

Address: _____

City_____ State_____ Zip _____

Please send this form with check or money order to
Filibuster Press, 55836 Riverdale Dr, Elkhart, IN 46514-1112.